# THE PILGRIM'S PROGRESS
## IN COLOUR

## JOHN BUNYAN

WITH COLOURING BY
JIM THORNTON

CHURCH HOME GROUP RESOURCES LTD

THE PILGRIM'S PROGRESS IN COLOUR



978-0-9532398-6-3

First Published 2012 by
Church Home Group Resources Ltd
25 Castle Street, Hertford, Herts SG14 1HH, UK E: info@CHGRL.org



Printed in Great Britain by
The Berforts Group
Stevenage

# THE PILGRIM'S PROGRESS
## IN COLOUR

***From This World,
To That Which is to Come***

*... This Book is writ in such a Dialect,*
*As may the minds of listless Men affect:*
*It seems a Novelty, and yet contains*
*Nothing but sound and honest Gospel strains.*
*Woulds't thou divert thy self from Melancholy?*
*Wouldst thou be pleasant, yet be far from folly?*
*Wouldst thou read Riddles, and their Explanation,*
*Or else be drowned in thy Contemplation?*
*Dost thou love picking-meat? Or wouldst thou see*
*A Man i'th Clouds, and hear him speak to thee?*
*Wouldst thou in a moment laugh and weep?*
*Wouldst thou lose thy self, and catch no harm?*
*And find thy self again without a charm?*
*Wouldst read thy self, and read thou knowest not what,*
*And yet know whether thou art blest or not,*
*By reading the same Lines? O then come hither,*
*And lay my Book, thy Head, and Heart together.*

# INTRODUCTION

Some of my friends get upset when I suggest that Bunyan's Pilgrim's Progress is unreadable. What I mean by this is that if you are reading it to find encouragement for your spiritual journey, it is hard work. First, you have to translate it into normal English, then you have to rethink it from the 17$^{th}$ to the 21$^{st}$ Century, and then you have to work out if what you have read is any help.

Many people have done a translation job. Some have done update jobs, but the problem is how to make Bunyan's one dimensional characters into real people. Who of your friends and acquaintances would you say is most like Mr BY-ENDS? Or the INTERPRETER? Or FAITHFUL? Is it better to flesh the characters out, or do they work only as cardboard cut-outs, spelled out in capital letters?

There has been a renewed interest in Puritan theology in some parts of the church. What did they believe about the Holy Spirit? Where is the Spirit in Pilgrim's Progress? What does 'sin' mean to this generation, and is it something they worry about? If not, does Bunyan have anything to say to this generation other than trying to frighten them with the threat of hell? What would John Bunyan say to Hans Kung or Rob Bell or Marcus Borg or Steve Chalke? Does it matter?

Well, I myself would rather like to know the answers to some of these questions, and I suspect some others might as well, so I set out on this journey with seven points in mind:

1. This book has had a profound effect on the spiritual journey of probably millions of Christians since it was written. If it has indeed become unreadable, then if it became more accessible, would it help a new generation in any way?

2. I am sure you are not interested in my view on what Bunyan meant by certain comments. I am sure you want to know exactly what Bunyan said. Every so often you will find words in *italics* which are the direct quotes from the original. These may be phrases which are better left as he wrote them, or where I am uncertain as to precisely what he meant. Mostly they are there just to reassure you that we are still with Bunyan.

3. I have taken the liberty of trying to make some of the characters more human and real, but given the constraints, this has inevitably simply meant making them two dimensional rather than one dimensional. I have kept with a tradition of having the person's name in capital letters.

4. I have tried to paint some coloured background, and I have tried to break up the lengthy dialogues, but the purpose is always to keep the interest going rather than insert some theology.

5. So I have followed James Patterson and broken the work up into short chapters, trying to end each chapter with a page-turner.

6. I have changed the Bible Quotations from Authorised Version to 21st Century King James Version, and put them in **Eras Bold ITC**. The whole work is riddled with Biblical quotations, so I have put all the References in Bunyan's Margins into an Appendix, listed by chapters.

7. Finally, the work that Jorj Kowszun, CHGR and I do is aimed at helping provide Church Home Groups with useful material for Christians of all traditions, especially thinking evangelical pente-catholic Christians (© N T Wright). The Coffee Breaks have some suggestions to get a discussion going.

Jim Thornton, February 2012

# CONTENTS

# 1 A MAN IN A MESS

*As I walked through the wilderness of this world,* I found myself in a little local difficulty. The bed in the Police Cell was pretty basic, but I was able to sleep, and I had a dream.

I dreamed I saw a man in jeans and a tee-shirt standing at a bus stop. He was carrying a huge rucksack, strapped tightly to him with chains and padlocks.

He held a Book, and I saw him open the Book and begin to read. He climbed on the bus when it arrived, and carried on reading during the bus journey. I could see he was beginning to get a bit emotional.

As he stepped off the bus, overcome with distress, he cried out: *"What shall I do?"*

In this state, he walked home and tried not to let his wife and children see how upset he was. But he could not hide his feelings from them for long. They stared at him as he sat on a stool in the kitchen with his head in his hands, the rucksack weighing him down.

"I am in a mess," he said. "This weight is more than I can bear. And I am convinced that this place is to be destroyed, along with everyone in it. I have to find some way for us all to escape."

His family looked at him with horror.

They did not think for one minute that his doomsday prediction was true, but they were panicking at the thought that he might be having a nervous breakdown. His wife told him to have a hot bath and go to bed, and she told the children to go and watch television.

But he couldn't sleep. He tossed and turned all night, sighing and groaning. In the morning, he staggered down for breakfast and when his daughter asked him how he felt, he said, "Terrible".

"I'm so worried," he went on. "We're in real danger and I don't know what to do..." His wife said sharply that the children were late for school and they had to go.

For days he was in a state of permanent anxiety.

His wife thought he should go to the doctor and get a prescription for Prozac; his mother came round with her medicinal prune and Brussels sprouts cheesecake; his brother said he just needed to go out for a pint; his sister-in-law suggested aromatherapy; his father told him to pull himself together.

But I could see that none of their well-meant prescriptions were helping a man with a *sick soul.* After a while they got annoyed, and stopped talking to him.

"Let him stew in his own juice," they said.

He shut himself in his garden shed, sometimes pitying his family and their short-sightedness, sometimes pitying himself. He went for long walks in the field behind his house, all the time carrying the heavy rucksack, turning over his thoughts in his mind and occasionally stopping to read and to pray.

I was watching him like this, pacing the field and reading his Book, growing more and more distracted, when he suddenly stopped and burst out: *"What shall I do to be saved?"*

He stared this way and that, like a cornered animal not knowing which way to run. An elderly man, out walking his dog, paused and came across to him.

"Are you all right?" asked the man, as his dog sniffed rabbit trails in the grass. "My name is EVANGELIST. What's the matter?"

The man took a deep breath and opened up to him. "This Book," he said, "tells me I'm condemned to die and face judgment. I don't want to die and I'm terrified of being judged."

"What's so bad about death?" asked EVANGELIST. "Life is so full of troubles, why not have an end to them?"

"Because this burden on my back is so heavy, it will sink me lower than the grave and drag me down to hell," he said. "And if I have to face judgment, I'm afraid that I'll be condemned."

"Well," said EVANGELIST, "why are you standing here? Why don't you come to a meeting I am speaking at next week?"

He reached into his pocket and pulled out a printed flyer with details, and gave it to him. The title of the talk was: "*Flee From the Wrath to Come!*"

"That's it!" said the man. "I feel I must run – but where to?"

EVANGELIST pointed across the fields. "Can you see a small gate over there?"

"No," said the man, squinting into the distance.

"Can you see a shining light?"

"Yes, I think so."

"Well keep that light in your line of vision and head towards it. As you get nearer, you will see a little wicket gate. When you knock, you'll be told what to do."

"Thank you," said the man. "I couldn't have known that without you."

"No, indeed," said EVANGELIST, and he put his dog on the lead and went off.

So I saw the man shift his heavy rucksack on his shoulders and start to run. He wasn't far from his house, and at that point his youngest son came out to call him in for tea. "Dad!" he shouted, "Dad! Where are you going? It's spaghetti carbonara!"

But the man ran on, putting his fingers in his ears and shouting out: *"Life, life! Eternal life!"*

The neighbours heard the noise and came out into their back gardens to see what was going on. Everyone was staring at the man, who was keeping up a good pace despite his heavy load.

"Faster, faster!" jeered one.

"He's heading for a heart attack," called another.

"Do something!" begged the man's wife.

# 2 EVERYBODY NEEDS GOOD NEIGHBOURS...

Two of the neighbours, who were members of the Hash House Harriers, reckoned they could easily overtake him and so set off.

Eventually, they caught up with him.

"That's enough," said OBSTINATE, a down-to-earth ex-miner from Yorkshire. "Time to get back."

"Your kids are quite upset," said PLIABLE, a popular guy who was everybody's friend.

"I can't go back," the man insisted. "We're all living in the City of Destruction – I see that now. If we die there, we'll sink into endless misery. Come on. I think there's a better way. Come with me."

"What!" gasped OBSTINATE. "Leave? When I've just joined the golf club and bought a Lexus?"

"The life I am seeking has much more to offer than that," said the man, whose name was CHRISTIAN. "Come with me and see if I am right."

"What's so great about this life you're running off to?" asked OBSTINATE. "And why do you have to leave everything behind?"

CHRISTIAN replied: "I am looking for something that will last for ever, something pure and precious. I believe it is waiting for me, if I seek it out. My Book says so – here, read it."

"You know where you can put your Book," said OBSTINATE. "Are you going to stop this nonsense and come back with us or not?"

"No," said CHRISTIAN, *"because I have laid my hand to the plough."*

"Come on, PLIABLE, let's go," said OBSTINATE. "The man's off his head and there's no telling him. He reckons he knows better than anyone else."

But PLIABLE was not so sure. "Let's not criticise," he said. "Suppose he's right? There might be something in what he says. I'm inclined to go with him."

"Forget it!" said OBSTINATE. "Can't you see he's a bit bananas? Who knows where he'll take you? See sense man, and come home."

"No, come with me PLIABLE," said CHRISTIAN. "You're right. There has to be more to life than football and the lottery. It's all here in my Book – the person who wrote this was willing to die for the truth of what it says."

Turning to OBSTINATE, PLIABLE said: "I have changed my mind. I'm going with CHRISTIAN."

OBSTINATE called him something unrepeatable, turned and ran back towards the houses.

"Well – let's go," said PLIABLE to CHRISTIAN. "Do you actually know the way?"

"A bloke named EVANGELIST gave me directions," CHRISTIAN said. "He told me to head for a little gate, where we can get instructions on how to go on."

*"Come then, good neighbour, let us be going,"* said PLIABLE.

They set off together towards the gate, and CHRISTIAN told PLIABLE how pleased he was to have company. The path led down a gentle hill and entered some woods.

"I'm really excited about this, too," said PLIABLE. "But come on CHRISTIAN, there's just the two of us now so you can tell me, what exactly is this precious stuff we're going to find?"

"I have an idea, but it's hard to put into words," replied CHRISTIAN. "It's all here in this Book."

"And you reckon it's true?" asked PLIABLE.

"I do, because God would not lie to us."

"So? What does it say?"

CHRISTIAN took a deep breath and said: "The Book talks of an endless Kingdom, where we will live for eternity. We will have crowns of glory and clothes that shine like the sun."

"Wow," said PLIABLE. "What else?"

"There will be no more crying or sorrow there," said CHRISTIAN. "The Lord of that Kingdom *will wipe away all tears from our eyes.*"

"Amazing," said PLIABLE. "And?"

"We will be surrounded by Seraphim and Cherubim – glorious angels that dazzle the eyes. We will meet all the tens of thousands of people who have gone before us to the kingdom, all *loving and holy, every one walking in the sight of God and standing in his presence with acceptance for ever.* We shall see *the elders with their golden crowns* and *Holy virgins with their golden harps*."

"That is so cool," said PLIABLE.

"We will also see all those who suffered for their faith in this world, tortured and martyred, burned at the stake or devoured by lions in the Coliseum, all because they loved God. We will see them made whole and immortal."

"Wow," said PLIABLE, again. "And how do we get a piece of the action – gold crowns, immortality and that?"

"The Book says if we want it, God will *bestow it upon us freely*."

"All right!" said PLIABLE. "Let's go. Come on, speed up."

"It's not easy," said CHRISTIAN, "with this heavy pack on my back. But I'll do my best."

While they walked along, deep in conversation, they left the cool of the woods and entered some meadows running beside a river.

They were not looking where they were going and all of a sudden they found themselves sinking into soft mud. They squelched on but were quickly up to their knees in black mire. Unable to keep their balance, they floundered in the foul-smelling muck.

With every struggle, CHRISTIAN sank deeper into the slime, his heavy pack dragging him down.

# 3 BOGGED DOWN

"This is disgusting!" yelled PLIABLE, his Ted Baker sweatshirt daubed with mud. "What have you got us into?"

"I don't know," said CHRISTIAN. "Can you give me a hand?"

"No way!" said PLIABLE. "Is this the shining happiness your precious Book promises? We've only just started and already we're up to our necks in a bog. I'm not hanging around to see what other delights are in store before we reach the end of our journey. If I get out of this, mate, you're welcome to your eternal Kingdom."

He wallowed around and, with a couple of enormous heaves, managed to crawl out of the mire and get back on the path they had just come along. Then, without a backward glance to CHRISTIAN, he squelched off home.

CHRISTIAN was determined not to give up. He waded laboriously through the mud in the direction of the gate and tried desperately to find dry land. But with the leaden weight of his rucksack holding him back, he could not pull himself out.

Then I saw a fisherman walk across the field to him, his rod in one hand and his green umbrella in the other.

"What are you doing in there?" asked the fisherman, whose name was HELP.

"I fell in. I'm trying to get to that gate over there," said CHRISTIAN. "A man called EVANGELIST told me this was the best way, to escape the wrath to come. But I ended up in the mud."

"Why didn't you use the stepping stones?" asked HELP.

CHRISTIAN looked back and sure enough there were a few boulders forming a path through the marsh.

"I was in such a panic, I didn't see them," he admitted.

HELP stretched out his umbrella, CHRISTIAN grasped it and, with some effort, the fisherman pulled him on to dry land.

CHRISTIAN sat there, feeling filthy and foolish. HELP poured him a cup of coffee from his Thermos.

"What is this place?" asked CHRISTIAN.

"The Slough of Despond. The Bog of Despair, you might call it," said HELP.

"It's disgusting – why hasn't it been drained and filled in? It's a danger to travellers."

"They've tried, but it can't be done," HELP said. "It's a sump that collects all the misery of sin."

HELP sat down on a rock. "When someone, like yourself, wakes up to the truth of the human condition, you start to find in your *soul many fears and doubts.* You get anxious and discouraged. These fears float like scum on top of the new-found self-knowledge. And all that scum and filth pools here, and creates this trap of despair, into which you and your fair-weather friend walked.

"The authorities have done their best to resolve the problem of this swamp. In fact, for the past two thousand years there has been a reclamation programme and countless lorry loads of good instructions have been brought down here, so the treacherous ground can be filled in with solid advice. The engineers told me they used the best materials they could source from all round the world. But the bog swallows it all. It's still the Slough of Despond and it always will be."

HELP stood up and pointed back towards the wood.

"There is a safe way through it, if you use the stepping stones. However, this place spews out so much muck that the path gets hidden, especially in bad weather. Travellers become disorientated and discouraged and forget to look for the steps. But you are through it now and I assure you that the ground is good once you pass through the gate."

CHRISTIAN looked relieved and shifted his backpack, ready to set off again.

Meanwhile I saw in my dream that PLIABLE had arrived home and was telling everyone at the pub what had happened. Some people thought he had got what he deserved for setting out with CHRISTIAN; others laughed at him for being scared of a bit of mud.

But PLIABLE grew bolder and told them of the horrendous dangers CHRISTIAN had dragged him into, until they all came round to his side and agreed that CHRISTIAN was a fool.

CHRISTIAN was back on the path, walking alone now, when bumping along the track towards him came an Orkney Grey Range Rover. At the wheel was Mr WORLDLY WISEMAN, the successful owner of a chain of estate agents in the prosperous Town of Carnal Policy, not far from CHRISTIAN's home in the City of Destruction.

Gossip about CHRISTIAN and his journey had spread, and WORLDLY WISEMAN had come to find CHRISTIAN himself.

# 4 ADVICE FROM AN ESTATE AGENT

As CHRISTIAN struggled along, out of breath, WORLDLY WISEMAN stopped the car and wound down the window. “Hullo, old chap – that looks like heavy going,” he said.

“It is,” admitted CHRISTIAN. “But I’m told that once I reach the wicket gate, I’ll be able to put my pack down.”

WORLDLY WISEMAN shut off the engine and got out of the car. “Are you on your own? Where are your wife and children?” he asked.

“They’re at home. I’ve been so weighed down with this burden that I couldn’t take any pleasure in family life. I feel I’m better off on my own.”

WORLDLY WISEMAN sighed and looked concerned. “Can I give you a bit of advice, old chap?” he said, sympathetically.

“Absolutely,” said CHRISTIAN. “I need all the help I can get.”

“Then you’ve got to get rid of that rucksack. It’s the source of all your troubles. You’ll never have any peace of mind until it’s gone, and you’ll never be able to enjoy all the good things in life the Lord has provided.”

“I’d love to be rid of it!” CHRISTIAN cried. “But I can’t take it off myself and nobody else has been able to lift it off my shoulders.

As I said, I'm heading towards that gate because there, I'm told, I'll be able to put down this load."

"Who told you that?"

"Someone I met out walking his dog – EVANGELIST his name was. He seemed wise and trustworthy."

WORLDLY WISEMAN sighed again and shook his head. "Very poor advice, I'm afraid. Quite irresponsible, really. He has sent you along the most difficult path imaginable, in fact there is *not a more dangerous and troublesome way in the world* – and believe me, I know these parts. Property's my game, you see."

He looked CHRISTIAN up and down. "By the state of you, I'd guess you've already wandered into the bog. And that's just the first of the obstacles ahead, if you follow that man's path.

"Now listen. You're a young man. I've knocked around a bit so perhaps you'll hear me out. If you carry on the way you're going, you're heading for exhaustion, pain, *hunger, perils, nakedness, swords, lions, dragons, darkness and, in a word, death*. Is that worth it, just on the word of an old codger with a dog?"

CHRISTIAN was taken aback, especially by the idea of dragons. But that seemed so far-fetched, while the weight of his rucksack was all too real and the straps were cutting deep into his shoulders.

"This load on my back is worse than anything you've mentioned," he sighed. "To be honest, I don't care how many lions I meet, as long as I can get rid of this burden."

"But how did you come to be carrying the thing in the first place?" asked his new friend.

*"By reading this Book in my hand,"* said CHRISTIAN.

Mr WORLDLY WISEMAN shook his head sadly. "I thought so," he said. "I've seen this happen to other inexperienced types. You read this Book, most of it is over your head, you haven't the training to deal with it and you get distracted by all sorts of half-baked ideas.

"The trouble is, chaps get one of these ideas fixed in their head – and this seems to have been what happened to you – and they launch themselves on some desperate venture, without really knowing what they're after."

"I know what I'm after," said CHRISTIAN, firmly. "I want to get rid of this burden."

"So why do it the hard way?" said Mr WORLDLY WISEMAN, "when I can show you a much easier way, and nearby, too. Follow my directions and not only will you avoid danger, you'll soon find *safety, friendship and content*."

CHRISTIAN felt cheered. "Tell me," he said.

"Just over there is the Village of Morality, a lovely little neighbourhood. A solicitor lives there – a very sound chap called LEGALITY. He has an excellent reputation. His particular speciality is helping people like yourself get the loads off their shoulders. Not only that, but he's a very good counsellor to those who have gone *somewhat crazed in their wits with their burdens*. Talk to him and you'll feel much better.

"His office is less than a mile from here and if he's not in, I'm sure you'll find his son, a very nice young man, name of CIVILITY, who is just as good as his father.

"Let them get rid of your burden and then, if you don't want to go back to your old home town – and frankly, I'd advise you not to, the place is on the slide – why not call your wife and get her to come over to the village?

"She'll love it, and so will the children. It's a very sought after location and there are some highly desirable properties there, at excellent prices. It's a jolly comfortable lifestyle in the village and you won't be disappointed in the neighbours. You'll find a very good class of person lives in the Village of Morality."

CHRISTIAN didn't know what to do. But the more he thought about it, the more he concluded that, if what WORLDLY WISEMAN said was true, his best course of action was to head for the Village of Morality.

"Which is the way to LEGALITY's place then?" he asked.

"You see this steep hill? Turn off this road and take the path straight over the hill. The first house you come to before the village is his. Can't miss it."

Mr WORLDLY WISEMAN clapped CHRISTIAN on the back and got back in his car.

"Best of luck, old chap," he laughed, and he revved the engine and pulled off, his back wheels spraying CHRISTIAN with a little more mud.

CHRISTIAN looked for the way up the hill. A few yards ahead he saw a sign for a footpath and thought that must be it, so he turned off the road and took the path.

Sure enough, it soon began to climb.

At first, CHRISTIAN felt reassured that he was following WORLDLY WISEMAN's instructions correctly but, after a while, the path was so steep that he was struggling to catch his breath.

The pack on his back seemed to get heavier and heavier.

CHRISTIAN climbed for what felt like a long time, but he seemed no nearer the top. The path was narrow, with treacherous loose stones under foot and a menacing overhang of rock above his head. Storm clouds were beginning to gather overhead, and gusts of wind would catch his backpack and make him lose his balance.

From time to time, a cascade of stones would come rattling down the hillside, missing CHRISTIAN by inches, and he began to be seriously afraid that the hill would come down on his head in a landslide.

As he paused, struggling with his backpack and uncertain whether to continue, lightning split the sky and struck the hill.

CHRISTIAN broke out in a cold sweat, not knowing whether he was going to be buried by a rock fall or cremated by a thunderbolt.

# 5 THE HAZARDOUS HILL

He realised with a sinking heart that taking WORLDLY WISEMAN's advice was the worst decision he could have made.

Just then he heard a gruff bark. He looked up and saw a dog trotting down the path towards him. It looked familiar. Then he saw its owner and recognised him as the elderly man, EVANGELIST, whom he had met at the start of his journey.

CHRISTIAN went red with shame, feeling stupid at being found so obviously in trouble and so far off the path which this man had advised. Sure enough, as he drew near, EVANGELIST looked at CHRISTIAN *with a severe and dreadful countenance.* "What are you doing here?" he said bluntly.

CHRISTIAN couldn't think of anything to say.

"Aren't you the man I met near the City of Destruction? You were in some distress, as I remember."

"Yes," admitted CHRISTIAN. "That was me."

"And didn't I tell you the way to the little wicket gate?"

"You did."

"Then what on earth are you doing here? How did you lose your way so quickly? You're going in completely the wrong direction."

CHRISTIAN explained to him about meeting the helpful businessman with the Range Rover, how he had been struggling with his heavy pack and the man had suggested someone who could help him put the burden down. “I told him I was heading for the wicket gate, but *he said that he would shew me a better way, and short, not so attended with difficulties as the way, sir, that you set me in.*

“But once I started climbing this hill, it turned out to be very steep and quite hazardous. So I stopped and now, to be honest, I don’t know what to do.”

CHRISTIAN slowly sank down onto a rock beside the path, and EVANGELIST sat beside him.

“Let’s have a look at the words of God,” he said. CHRISTIAN found himself trembling: he dreaded what EVANGELIST was going to say. The old man was patient, but firm. He took CHRISTIAN’s Book, and thumbed through to find the text he wanted.

“Listen to this, from the letter to the Hebrews, chapter 12 verse 25. It’s a warning that we must not ignore Christ’s words: **‘See that ye refuse not Him that speaketh, for if they escaped not who refused Him that spoke on earth, much more shall we not escape if we turn away from Him that speaketh from Heaven.’** The Book also tells us here in Hebrews chapter 10 verse 38: **‘Now the just shall live by faith; but if any man draw back, My soul shall have no pleasure in him.’**

“I’m afraid that this means you,” EVANGELIST continued. “You decided not to listen. *You drew back your foot from the way of peace* and took this other path, putting yourself at enormous risk of losing everything.”

When he realised what he had done, CHRISTIAN felt a bit faint. He buried his face in his hands: "I've ruined everything," he moaned.

But EVANGELIST laid a kindly hand on his shoulders. "Don't talk like that – have faith," he said. *"All manner of sin and blasphemy shall be forgiven unto men; be not faithless, but believing."*

CHRISTIAN took a deep breath and felt a little calmer. "I am ready to listen," he said. "Why did that man send me this way?"

"His name is WORLDLY WISEMAN," said EVANGELIST. "We know each other of old and he is always trying to obstruct me and lead people astray.

"He loves the things of this world. He is always looking for a comfortable life but he likes to make a show of godliness, too. So he goes to church in the Village of Morality, because there they preach respectability and upstanding behaviour, without ever talking of the cross. They will tell you there's no need for suffering: all you need to do is abide by the moral rules.

"There are three reasons why Mr WORLDLY WISEMAN's advice is utterly wrong. Firstly, he directed you off the right path. Secondly, he tried to make you reject the cross. Finally, he sent you this way, up Mount Sinai, which is a harsh and dangerous route."

"But he wasn't such a bad person," CHRISTIAN said.

"You're wrong there," EVANGELIST replied. "Think about what I just said. First, he sent you off the true path – he maintained that his advice was better than God's advice.

*"The Lord says, 'Strive to enter in at the strait gate',* and that's the gate I pointed you towards. It's in your Book: **'Enter ye in at the strait gate, for wide is the gate and broad is the way that leadeth to destruction, and many there be who go**

**in thereat. Because strait is the gate, and narrow is the way which leadeth unto life, and few there be that find it.'**

"That little wicket gate?" asked CHRISTIAN, puzzled. "It looked a bit crooked to me."

"Strait meaning narrow, like the Straits of Gibraltar," explained EVANGELIST. "It's not easy to get through, but I was helping you, which is why WORLDLY WISEMAN did you such a bad turn and why you should regret listening to him.

"And then, secondly, he tried to make you despise the cross."

"What do you mean?" asked CHRISTIAN.

"He was offering you an easy life, trying to convince you that suffering and hardship was unnecessary. But the Lord says to find life, you have to lose it, not indulge it. It's in your Book: **'If any man come to Me and hate not his father and mother, and wife and children, and brethren and sisters, yea, and his own life also, he cannot be My disciple.'**

"Remember Moses: he could have had all the treasures of Egypt at the Pharoah's court, but he gave that up to share the suffering of the captive Israelites. Without death of self and the death on the cross, there can be no life as it is meant to be."

"Then, thirdly, *thou must hate his setting of thy feet in the way that leadeth to the ministration of death.* Think about the person he pointed you towards."

"But why is it wrong for me to be going to see LEGALITY?" asked CHRISTIAN. "Surely if he can get this burden off my back, that is as good as being able to put it down at the wicket gate, as you promised?"

"He can't do any such thing," said EVANGELIST. "He has never been able to help anyone off with their backpack and he won't be able to help you. No man living can be rid of his burden simply by obeying the Ten Commandments.

"And there's more. Abiding by the law doesn't set you free: it simply keeps you in slavery. *Mr LEGALITY is a cheat, and for his son, CIVILITY, notwithstanding his simpering looks, he is but a hypocrite and cannot help thee.*"

Then EVANGELIST prayed to God for confirmation of what he had said, and with that there came words and fire out of the mountain under which poor CHRISTIAN was standing. This made his hair stand on end. He heard the words from Galatians 3:10: **'For as many as are of the works of the law are under the curse; for it is written: "Cursed is every one who continueth not in all things which are written in the book of the law to do them."'**

CHRISTIAN was in despair. He realised what a mistake it had been to try and go this way. Convinced that nothing could save him now, he cursed WORLDLY WISEMAN and called himself an idiot for listening to the man.

"I can see now he was only interested in material comforts. Why did I think his way was better than yours?" he said, miserably.

But, he thought, EVANGELIST was still there to help him. "What do you think, sir?" he said. "Is there any hope? Can I carry on to the wicket gate or will I be turned away? I'm sorry I listened to that man's advice, but I hope I can be forgiven for that mistake."

"Well," said EVANGELIST. "You actually made two grave mistakes – not only did you abandon the right way, but you then took the forbidden way.

"But the man at the gate is kind and won't turn you away. Just stick to the path this time."

So CHRISTIAN shifted the rucksack on his shoulders and prepared to go back and pick up the path again. EVANGELIST hugged him, handed him a booklet called 'The Four Spiritual Laws', and *gave him one smile and bid him godspeed.*

CHRISTIAN walked purposefully back towards the wicket gate, determined not to speak to anyone he met, in case he should once again be sent off course. He hurried like a man *treading on forbidden ground*, knowing he wouldn't feel safe until he was back on the path EVANGELIST had showed him.

At last he reached the gate, and saw that to get through it there was a small door within the bigger framework. Written above this door were the words: *'Knock; and it shall be opened unto you'.* So he knocked, several times.

As he waited, he turned over some words in his head that had the beginnings of a song:

*May I now enter here? Will he within*
*Open to sorry me, though I have been*
*An undeserving rebel? Then shall I*
*Not fail to sing his lasting praise on high.*

# 6 THE KEEPER OF THE WICKET GATE

After a while he heard steps approaching from the other side of the narrow door. CHRISTIAN peered through a small grating at eye level, and a man with a solemn face came into view.

In his morning dress, top hat and serious manner, he reminded CHRISTIAN of the doorman at Claridges. He announced his name as GOODWILL, and with great politeness asked CHRISTIAN who he was, where he had come from, and what he would like?

"*Here is a poor burdened sinner,"* said CHRISTIAN. "I have just walked from the City of Destruction; *but am going to Mount Zion, that I may be delivered from the wrath to come.* I believe I need to go through this wicket gate, if you will let me in."

GOODWILL replied: "Indeed, sir, you are most welcome," and he pulled back a bolt and opened the little door.

As CHRISTIAN began to struggle through with his heavy rucksack, GOODWILL grabbed him by the arm and pulled him quickly through the doorway. "Hey, what's that for?" yelped CHRISTIAN.

"I do apologise, sir, but if you look above the trees you will see the gatehouse of a castle. *Beelzebub is the captain* there," said

GOODWILL, "and his devilish crew often take pot-shots at people who arrive at the wicket gate, in the hope of killing a few before they can get in."

"Well," said CHRISTIAN, shaking with relief. *"I rejoice and tremble."*

GOODWILL closed the door, and led CHRISTIAN towards a bench where there was a picnic hamper of the finest quality, complete with china cups and linen napkins. "Please partake of some tea with me, Mr..."

"CHRISTIAN," said CHRISTIAN. He sat down while GOODWILL poured a steaming cup of Lapsang Souchong from a solar powered Samovar.

"May I ask who told you to come here?" continued GOODWILL.

CHRISTIAN explained about meeting EVANGELIST. "He said you would let me know what to do next."

*"An open door is set before thee and no man can shut it,"* said GOODWILL.

CHRISTIAN took heart from this and began to feel that he was at last beginning to reap some benefits from all the difficulties and dangers he had gone though.

"But tell me: why are you travelling alone?" asked the doorkeeper.

"My family and neighbours just couldn't get it. They couldn't see the state we were in," said CHRISTIAN. "When I set off, my wife and children shouted after me to come back, but I put my fingers in my ears and carried on."

CHRISTIAN told GOODWILL about OBSTINATE and PLIABLE and how PLIABLE had gone back home after he'd fallen in the Slough of Despond. "He said I could keep my eternal Kingdom."

GOODWILL pondered, and then said, “Poor man. Did he really count the promise of heavenly glory not worth the risk of a few difficulties?”

“To be honest, I am no better than PLIABLE,” admitted CHRISTIAN. “Yes, he went back home, but I also turned off the path after listening to that devious estate agent, WORLDLY WISEMAN.”

GOODWILL smiled and poured more tea. “I imagine he attempted to persuade you to choose the easy life advocated by Mr LEGALITY. They are a notorious pair of frauds. Did you follow his advice?”

“I tried,” said CHRISTIAN. “I took the path over the hill to LEGALITY’s house, but the rock face seemed about to collapse on top of me, and I stopped.”

“*That mountain has been the death of many, and will be the death of many more,*” said GOODWILL. “You were fortunate to escape.”

“I might not have done,” CHRISTIAN replied, “but as I was wondering what on earth to do, EVANGELIST came along, and God was merciful to me.” CHRISTIAN paused, suddenly realising what a narrow escape he had had, and feeling overcome with shame at his stupidity.

“Perhaps I deserved to be swept away by the landslide, rather than standing here telling you this, but I am so thankful that I’ve reached the gate and you have let me in.”

GOODWILL stood up and said: “We do not condemn anyone for what they have done in the past. No one is turned away. Come with me, CHRISTIAN, and I will show you the next stage of your journey.”

He led CHRISTIAN to a country lane. It was narrow, but stretched away into the distance as straight as a ruler. "This is the road you must follow," he said. "It was originally built by *patriarchs, prophets, Christ, and his apostles,* and it is as straight as any made by the Romans. This is the way you must go."

CHRISTIAN was a little doubtful. "Are you sure there are no twists and turns to make me lose my way?" he asked.

"There are many turnings off the road, and they are *crooked and wide*: but you can always tell the right road because it is *straight and narrow.*

In my dream I saw CHRISTIAN ask GOODWILL if he did not have anything handy in his picnic hamper to get his backpack off. "A sharp knife? Scissors? Bolt-cutters?" he asked, hopefully. "This thing is really weighing me down."

But GOODWILL smiled and handed him only some sandwiches from the picnic basket. "Carry your burden a bit longer. When you come to the place of deliverance it will fall off your back of its own accord. But for now, press on down this lane, and after a few miles you will come to the house of the INTERPRETER. Knock on his door and he will show you *excellent things.*"

So CHRISTIAN stepped out into the lane, sad to leave a good friend.

After a couple of hours CHRISTIAN came to the first houses of a village. He passed a school and a couple of shops and then entered a small square. The largest building on the square was a striking mock-Gothic edifice, with a clock tower and wide steps leading to an imposing entrance.

CHRISTIAN went up to it. Over the door was a sign, 'Village Museum and Art Gallery', but beside the door was also a brass plate which read, 'The Interpreter Foundation'.

This must be the place, he thought.

# 7 THE INTERPRETER

Through the main doors, he found himself in a large, stone-floored hall, where there was a polished oak reception desk.

Nervously, CHRISTIAN asked the receptionist if he could meet the INTERPRETER. She gave him a reassuring smile and pressed a bell.

After a few minutes a tall man appeared from an office behind the desk. He was bald, with a dark beard speckled with grey, and a fiercely intelligent look in his eyes. But to CHRISTIAN's relief there was a warmth about him, rather than the detached dryness of an academic. He shook hands with CHRISTIAN and asked him what he wanted.

"Sir," said CHRISTIAN. "I have travelled here from the City of Destruction and I'm on my way to Mount Zion. The doorman at the wicket gate told me that if I called in here I would be shown 'excellent things' to help me on my way."

The INTERPRETER smiled. "Yes indeed, we have a wealth of things to strengthen thinking evangelical pente-catholic pilgrims for the path ahead."

He considered for a minute, drumming his fingers on the reception desk, as a party of school children chattered through the hall and into a side gallery. "I think I will show you seven things. Let's start upstairs in the gallery with some of our oldest paintings."

## THE ART GALLERY

They walked up the main staircase, along a corridor, and into a small room that was dimly lit.

CHRISTIAN saw hanging on the wall in front of him a picture of a rather severe-looking man. The painter had depicted him with *eyes lifted up to heaven, the best of books in his hand, the law of truth was written upon his lips, the world was behind his back; it stood as if he pleaded with men, and a crown of gold did hang over his head.*

"Who is this?" asked CHRISTIAN.

The INTERPRETER smiled: "He is a father who gives birth to children and nurses them when born." CHRISTIAN was puzzled.

"Although his eyes are looking up, his work *is to know and unfold dark things to sinners;* you can see that he is trying to persuade those who read or hear his words," the INTERPRETER explained. "He has turned his back on his worldly career, and the crown hanging over his head shows you that*, slighting and despising the things that are present, for the love that he hath to his Master's service,* he is certain that in the next world he will have *glory for his reward*."

They stood silently contemplating the painting of St Paul for a few minutes. "I am showing you this painting first," said the INTERPRETER, "because this man is the only accredited guide for the difficult places you may come to on your journey. He is the only one authorised by the Lord of the place to which you are heading, so remember what I am showing you. Hold it in your mind in case you meet people on your journey who claim to be able to guide you, *but their way goes down to death."*

CHRISTIAN was thinking about this when the INTERPRETER said, "Let's move on".

## TRUE DIRT

He took CHRISTIAN back out into the corridor and opened the door of another room. CHRISTIAN was startled: it looked like a mouldering attic that had been left untouched for a century, littered with junk, and thick with grey dust.

A grumpy-looking janitor appeared with a broom, and began vigorously sweeping the room. This made matters worse: soon clouds of dust were swirling round, making CHRISTIAN cough. Then a young woman came in, with a plastic plant spray. She went round the room, spraying the dust with water and making it settle. This did the trick, and soon the dirt was swept up.

"What was that all about?" croaked CHRISTIAN, still trying to clear his throat.

"Think of the filthy room as like the heart of a person *that was never sanctified by the sweet grace of the gospel,"* said the INTERPRETER. "The dust and dirt are *original sin and inward corruptions,* which have turned the place into a complete shambles. The janitor represents the Law, and the young woman is the Gospel.

"Without the Gospel, when the Law got into the heart, it made things worse. It just stirred up the dirt so that we could hardly see or breathe. Instead of cleansing the heart, the Law actually encourages sin because the Law does not provide the strength that is needed to overcome temptation.

"But *when the Gospel comes in the sweet and precious influences thereof to the heart,* then just as the dirt is sorted, *so is sin vanquished and subdued; and the soul made clean through the faith of it, and consequently fit for the King of Glory to inhabit."*

CHRISTIAN was still coughing and the INTERPRETER offered him a throat sweet. "Sorry about that. But we do find real-life installations convey a powerful message," he said. "Can I now show you a triptych we have in the next room?"

## THE TRIPTYCH

They walked through an archway into the next gallery. On the side wall was an extraordinary blaze of colour. It was in the form of a mediaeval altar back, but looked as though it had been painted by Picasso, and touched up by Jackson Pollock on a particularly excitable day.

CHRISTIAN looked at the plaque beside the painting, which informed him the work was entitled 'PASSION and PATIENCE'.

"Look carefully at this first panel," said the INTERPRETER. "Here are two children. You can see that PASSION is having a tantrum."

"Looks like the artist was, too," said CHRISTIAN, "there's paint splodged everywhere. Why is PASSION so mad?"

"Their father has told them that they must wait until next year for the money their grandmother has left them," said the INTERPRETER. "PASSION wants it now, but PATIENCE is willing to wait. Look at this second panel: PASSION has been given £1,000 and is rushing off to spend it."

CHRISTIAN tried looking at it sideways, but was not convinced. "If you say so," he said,"and I suppose in this third panel he is having a wild rave?"

"No," said the INTERPRETER. "Look here in these dark colours, and you can see that the artist is showing that *he had lavished all away, and had nothing left him but rags."*

"And what does the artist want me to learn from this?"

"PASSION is all the people who only think about this world, while PATIENCE is those who live for the world to come. As you know, most people are only interested in having the good things in life now – *they cannot stay till next year, that is, until the next world, for their portion of good. That proverb, 'A bird in the hand is worth two in the bush,' is of more authority with them than are all the divine testimonies of the good of the world to come.* But as you saw, material goods quickly vanish and leave you with nothing – *so will it be with all such men at the end of this world."*

CHRISTIAN thought for a while, and then said: "So PATIENCE is the wise one, because he holds out for the best things, and he will be enjoying those, when PASSION has nothing but rags."

"There is a third point to remember," said the INTERPRETER, "and that is that *the glory of the next world will never wear out.* PASSION might mock PATIENCE, but PATIENCE will have the last laugh. He *that hath his portion first must needs have a time to spend it: but he that has his portion last must have it lastingly.*

"Remember the parable of Dives and Lazarus in Luke 16:25: **'But Abraham said, "Son, remember that thou in thy lifetime received thy good things, and likewise Lazarus evil things; but now he is comforted and thou art tormented."'"**

Folding his arms in front of the triptych, CHRISTIAN said: "So the painter wants me to know that it is better to wait for the good things to come, than to get stressed out keeping up with the neighbours?"

"Indeed," said the INTERPRETER. "The things we see will one day be dust, but the unseen things are for ever. That's the message of the painting, and pretty effective I think it is, too."

"If you say so," said CHRISTIAN doubtfully, "though I'm not a big fan of modern art."

"But the message of the painting is a very important one," insisted the INTERPRETER, "since the material world is a close neighbour to our natural appetites. Instinctively, we want material goods. But the eternal world is very different: we can't see it or touch it and we have to learn to value it. We must learn to desire what the next world offers.

"Now let us go downstairs and watch the children playing the video games. There is one in particular I want to show you."

## AN INTERACTIVE DISPLAY

Downstairs the INTERPRETER led the way into a gallery, which reminded CHRISTIAN of the time he spent an extremely noisy afternoon with his sons at the Science Museum. There was a range of hands-on displays, and children were absorbed in trying to balance blocks, make bridges, connect tubes, work pumps and generally re-create their own industrial revolution.

Along the back wall were a number of video game consoles, and the INTERPRETER led CHRISTIAN towards one surrounded by some cheering children. The game was to try and put out a blaze by guiding fire-fighters, fire engines, ladders and hosepipes to the necessary spot. The boy at the controls was struggling to get the fire under control. Every time he seemed to have it damped down, flames would break out at another place, and his friends would jeer and yell at him.

"What's the lesson here?" asked CHRISTIAN.

The INTERPRETER answered, *"This fire is the work of grace that is wrought in the heart."*

"You mean, it's not a blaze of destruction?" CHRISTIAN asked.

"No, indeed, the one trying to extinguish the fire is actually *the Devil.* As you see, he is not succeeding and if we wait until the end of the game, I'll show you why."

Just then 'Game Over' flashed on the screen and before another boy could muscle his way on to the seat, the INTERPRETER pressed a key on the controls, and displayed a bigger picture.

"Look," he said, "the player cannot see, but behind the scenes there is a man with a can of oil in his hand, with which he is constantly, secretly, feeding the flames."

"And who is this pyromaniac?" asked CHRISTIAN.

*The INTERPRETER answered, "This is Christ, who continually with the oil of his grace maintains the work already begun in the heart: by the means of which, notwithstanding what the Devil can do, the souls of his people prove gracious still.*

"And although you can see the man behind the scenes when I change the viewpoint from the keyboard, you will realise that *it is hard for the tempted to see how this work of grace is maintained in the soul."*

The boys were getting a bit restless, so the INTERPRETER hit 'return' and let them get on with the game.

## THE COURTYARD TABLEAU

"Let's go out into the courtyard," suggested the INTERPRETER.

So they walked down a passage to a door that opened into a sunny area at the rear of the museum, planted with exotic flowers, shrubs and foliage.

The far side of the courtyard was an extraordinary Georgian façade, in complete contrast to the neo-Gothic Museum. There was a ‘piano nobile’ floor at the top of a sweeping double staircase up from the courtyard. On a balcony over the wide entrance portico CHRISTIAN could see *certain persons walking, who were clothed all in gold.*

“Can we go over there?” asked CHRISTIAN.

They walked through the garden shrubbery towards the staircase, and CHRISTIAN could see a crowd on a sunken patio at the bottom of the main sweep. People wanted to get into the beautiful building, but seemed to be afraid of some security guards.

As they got closer, CHRISTIAN could see why: these guys looked mean. They wore black balaclavas and carried Uzi sub-machine guns, and several had jungle knives strapped to their belts. Standing menacingly at the bottom of each flight of steps, they were clearly on a mission to stop people entering.

On a patch of grass to the right of the patio was a man seated at a desk, with a large register in front of him. He was writing down the names of those who wanted to go in. As they watched, *CHRISTIAN saw a man of a very stout countenance come up to the man that sat there to write, saying, “Set down my name, sir.”*

His name was written down and the man headed for the staircase. “He’s going to have to be brave,” thought CHRISTIAN.

Suddenly the man produced from his pocket a gas grenade and threw it among the guards. Pulling on a gas mask, he rushed the special forces heavy mob, laying about him with his walking stick, which turned out to be a sword-stick.

The guards tried to overpower him, *but the man not at all discouraged, fell to cutting and hacking most fiercely. So, after he had received and given many wounds to those that attempted to keep him out, he cut his way through them all, and pressed forward into the palace; at which there was a pleasant voice heard from those that were within even of those that walked upon the top of the palace, saying,*

*"Come in! Come in!*
*Eternal glory thou shalt win."*

*So he went in, and was clothed with such garments as they.*

CHRISTIAN inwardly gave a cheer for the man's courage and determination. "I think I know what this means," he told the INTERPRETER confidently. "Maybe I ought now to be getting on my way."

"Not yet," said the INTERPRETER, "I have two last things to show you."

## THE PRISONER

They walked back into the museum, and along a corridor. At the end, they went through a door into what was obviously a much older building, and through a window CHRISTIAN could see the village square. The INTERPRETER led him into a very dark room, where there sat a man in an iron cage.

"This used to be the village gaol," said the INTERPRETER. "When we have a school visit, one of our staff dresses up as a prisoner and acts the part."

*Now, the man, to look on, seemed very sad. He sat with his eyes looking down to the ground; his hands folded together; and he sighed as if he would break his heart.* "What's his problem?" asked CHRISTIAN.

"Ask him," said the INTERPRETER.

CHRISTIAN coughed loudly to catch his attention and said, "Excuse me, but who are you?"

The man, whose name was BACKSLIDER, answered, *"I am what I was not once."*

"So what were you?" asked CHRISTIAN.

"I was once a very spiritual and holy person, in my eyes and the eyes of others, always ready to profess my beliefs to the world. As far as I was concerned, I was firmly on the road to heaven and felt a glow of satisfaction at the thought that I would certainly get there.

*"I am now a man of despair, and am shut up in it, as in this iron cage. I cannot get out; oh now, I cannot!"*

"How did you get like this?" asked CHRISTIAN.

"I became complacent. I let my guard down. I thought I could do no wrong so I didn't bother to rein in my desires. *I sinned against the Light of the World, and the goodness of God. I have grieved the Spirit, and he is gone. I tempted the Devil, and he is come to me. I have provoked God to anger, and he has left me. I have so hardened my heart that I cannot repent."*

CHRISTIAN turned to the INTERPRETER and whispered, "Is there no hope for him?"

"Ask him," said the INTERPRETER.

So CHRISTIAN said to BACKSLIDER, "Do you really think there is no hope for you? Surely Jesus will have mercy on you."

"No," said BACKSLIDER, *"I have crucified him to myself afresh.* I have treated Christ with contempt, I have despised his goodness, I have ignored his sacrifice. I have shut myself out from his promises and now all I know is the fearful threat of certain judgment and fiery punishment."

"How did you bring yourself into this condition?"

"Pursuing my greed and lust and selfish pleasures. It all seemed so satisfying at the time but now *every one of those things also bite me and gnaw me like a burning worm."*

CHRISTIAN was disturbed by how firmly the man was imprisoned in his impenetrable despair. "But surely all you need to do is repent and turn to Christ?"

*"God hath denied me repentance,"* said BACKSLIDER. *"His Word gives me no encouragement to believe: yea, himself hath shut me up in this iron cage; nor can all the men in the world let me out. Oh, eternity! eternity! How shall I grapple with the misery that I must meet with in eternity?"*

It seemed a light went out in CHRISTIAN's head, and he thought he felt cold air on the back of his neck. *"God help me to watch and be sober; and to pray,"* he said to himself. "This is bad stuff."

The INTERPRETER said: "Remember this man's despair as you travel on your journey, and now let us look at the last thing I want to show you."

## THE FILM CLIP

They walked back to the entrance hall, and the INTERPRETER led CHRISTIAN through the library and up some stairs into the Hexagon where there was a display dedicated to a well-known film director who had grown up in the village.

Apparently he had been inspired by French Nouvelle Vague and Italian Neorealism, and had been an important influence on Quentin Tarantino. At the centre of the display was a screen, and the INTERPRETER inserted a DVD into the player beneath it. "This is the film he considered to be his masterpiece," he said, and fast-forwarded through to a scene towards the end.

The picture was gloomy. It appeared to be a suburban bedroom at night; the camera zoomed slowly towards the double bed. Suddenly the bedclothes were thrown back and a young man sat up with a long look straight to camera of sheer terror.

“What’s woken him?” said CHRISTIAN. “Burglar? Husband come back earlier than expected?”

“Shush!” said the INTERPRETER. “His name’s UNREADY. The actor got an Oscar nomination for this.”

A young woman’s head appeared from under the duvet. She fumbled for the bedside lamp and switched it on. The man was hugging his knees, trembling.

“That was one hell of a dream,” he muttered.

The woman said nothing and reached for a packet of cigarettes beside the bed.

“There was, like, an electric storm – the sky was black. Lightning, flames. Then a trumpet blast and a guy sitting on a cloud, I’m not kidding. And then, like, I heard this voice, it was everywhere, saying, “*Arise ye dead and come to judgment*.”

The woman said nothing and lit a cigarette.

“And the rocks split apart and graves were opening and people were, like, rising out of the ground.”

The woman leaned back and blew out a plume of cigarette smoke.

“I guess some of the resurrected corpses were kinda pleased,” he went on. “But others were pretty unhappy. Then I was next to my old religious studies teacher from fifth grade, who was staring up at the guy on a cloud holding a book.

“Someone shouted ‘*Gather together the tares, the chaff and stubble, and cast them into the burning lake.’*

“And then – get this – a bottomless pit opened just where I was standing and it was like the mouth of a volcano spewing out smoke and lava. And then the voice said, *'Gather my wheat into the garner'.* And some people were caught up, right? Like in a twister? And carried away into the clouds.”

The woman yawned.

“*But I was left behind*!” cried the man. He leapt out of bed, naked, and rushed to the window, staring wildly out into the night.

“I wanted to hide, but there was no cover. And all the time the guy on the cloud was looking at me and all I could think of was all the bad things I'd ever done.”

He sat on the edge of the bed, his head in his hands. *“I thought that the Day of Judgment was come, and that I was not ready for it.* And you know what the really scary part was? That the angels had gathered these people up, but left me behind, standing there on the edge of the pit of hell. With the Judge in the cloud always with his eye on me, just – looking at me.”

“Weird,” said the woman, stubbing out her cigarette and switching off the light.

## SO WHAT DID YOU MAKE OF THAT?

The INTERPRETER turned off the DVD and led CHRISTIAN back into the main hall. “So what do you make of my seven ‘excellent things’?”

“Much food for thought,” said CHRISTIAN, *“and they put me in hope and fear.”*

They shook hands at the door, and the INTERPRETER smiled encouragingly at CHRISTIAN. *“Keep all things so in thy mind that they may be as a goad in thy sides, to prick thee forward in the way thou must go,”* he said. *“The Comforter be always with thee, good CHRISTIAN, to guide thee in the way that leads to the city.”*

So CHRISTIAN pushed through the doors, walked down the steps and back into the village square, ready to go on his way. He hummed to himself an adaptation of a song from a musical he had once performed in:

*Here I have seen things rare and profitable,*
*Things pleasant, dreadful, things to make me stable*
*In what I have begun to take in hand:*
*Then let me think on them, and understand*
*Wherefore they shew'd me were, and let me be*
*Thankful, O good Interpreter, to thee.*

CHRISTIAN walked out of the village square and back on to the right road.

Now I saw in my dream that on either side of the road was a wall, and the wall was called ‘Salvation’. CHRISTIAN was eager to get on and tried to break into a run, but the rucksack on his back still weighed heavily on him.

Nevertheless, he managed to quicken his pace and soon came to a low hill.

# 8 THE CROSS

On top of the hill stood a cross. In a hollow at the bottom of the hill was a tomb, with its lid open.

I saw CHRISTIAN climb up to the cross, and just as he reached it, the backpack slipped from his shoulders and fell to the ground, tumbling down the hill until it came to the stone sarcophagus. It dropped into the tomb and disappeared from sight.

*Then was CHRISTIAN glad and lightsome, and said, with a merry heart,*

*"He hath given me rest by his sorrow,*
*And life by his death."*

He paused for a while, to look and wonder. After struggling with his burden for so long, unable to take it off, he was surprised that simply the sight of the cross should relieve him of it. So he stood, gazing at the cross, tears in his eyes.

*Now, as he stood looking and weeping, behold three Shining Ones came to him, and saluted him with, "Peace be to thee!"*

The first one said to him: "Your sins are forgiven."

The second one took off his tatty mud-stained tee-shirt, and gave him new clothes to wear.

The third set a mark on his forehead and gave him a rolled parchment, with a seal on it. He told CHRISTIAN to look at this Roll as he travelled on, and to hand it in at the Celestial Gate. Then the Shining Ones left.

CHRISTIAN *gave three leaps for joy, and* went on his way singing.

*Thus far I did come loaden with my sin,*
*Nor could ought ease the grief that I was in,*
*Till I came hither: what a place is this!*
*Must here be the beginning of my bliss?*
*Must here the burden fall from off my back?*
*Must here the strings that bound it to me crack?*
*Bless'd Cross! Bless'd sepulchre! Bless'd rather be*
*The man that there was put to shame for me.*

# TIME FOR A COFFEE BREAK

Do you think of yourself as being on a journey through life?

Where do you think your own life journey will lead?

We all make assumptions about the meaning of life.
What assumptions do you make?
What would be the consequences of being wrong?

Do you know any people whose attitude to living you envy?
Why is their attitude better than yours?

What do you do when you feel dissatisfied with your lot?

Bunyan thought of the Stepping Stones across the Bog as being *the Promises of Forgiveness and Acceptance to life by Faith in Christ.* Have you come across any helpful promises in the Bible? If so, why would you believe them?

If Bunyan saw the wicket gate as Jesus, who is GOODWILL?

How do we decide who is a reliable interpreter of the Bible and of matters of faith and doctrine?

How can looking at the Cross lift a load?
How much do you need to know or understand before the Cross can be effective?

What do you think Bunyan meant the 'Roll' to represent?

'Shining Ones' make occasional appearances in Pilgrim's Progress. What do you think Bunyan had in mind? Do you think he met angels on his own 17th Century journey?

# 9 APPROACHING DIFFICULTY HILL

I saw then in my dream that a railway line ran along beside the road, and as he passed a gap in the wall, CHRISTIAN noticed a strange smell. Looking through the gap he saw three teenagers lying on the railway line. Something unusual had been smoked. Looking closer, he saw that they had tied their feet to the tracks. One of them was called SIMPLE, another SLOTH, and the third PRESUMPTION.

CHRISTIAN was alarmed and shouted over to them: "Hey, get off the tracks! Don't be daft, there'll be a train coming soon!" He hurried over to them, ready to help untie the knots.

But he got little response. SIMPLE said, "I see no danger, dude."

SLOTH roused himself, looked blearily at CHRISTIAN, then lay down again, mumbling, "Just a little more sleep."

PRESUMPTION said churlishly, "It's nothing to do with you. We can look after ourselves."

CHRISTIAN thought this was clearly untrue, but he could see there was no point arguing with them. He went back to the road, hoping they would come to their senses before the next train came along.

CHRISTIAN walked on, troubled that the young people had taken no notice of his warnings and the help he had offered.

As he was reflecting on this, two men came tumbling over the wall behind him on his left, like a pair of burglars making a getaway, and began to walk quickly along the road. *The name of the one was FORMALIST, and the name of the other HYPOCRISY.* FORMALIST wore a very smart three-piece pin-stripe suit, probably Gieves & Hawke, while HYPOCRISY was wearing a tracksuit.

As they caught up with him, CHRISTIAN said: "Hi there, are you travelling my way?"

They replied*: "We were born in the Land of Vain-Glory, and are going for praise to Mount Zion."*

"Really?" said CHRISTIAN, "That's where I am going too; but why did you climb over the wall? Surely you have to start at the wicket gate?"

"In Vain-Glory we find the wicket gate is too far away," said FORMALIST. "We usually take a short-cut and climb over the wall."

*"But will it not be counted a trespass against the Lord of the city whither we are bound, thus to violate his revealed will?"* asked CHRISTIAN.

"No worries," said HYPOCRISY. "In our country, people have been doing this for hundreds of years."

*"But," said CHRISTIAN, "will* your practice *stand a trial at law?"*

"What on earth are you talking about?" asked FORMALIST. "We are on the right road, so what does it matter how we got here? The important thing is that we are travelling together. Any impartial judge would acknowledge that since the citizens of Vain-Glory have been doing this since the reign of Richard III our custom has real validity. What makes you think you are any better than us?"

CHRISTIAN thought carefully before he replied. "I am following the rules laid down by my Master. You are making up your own rules. You came over the wall, like thieves, and I wouldn't be surprised if, when we reach our destination, you are judged to be less than honest. *You come in by yourselves without his direction, and shall go out by yourselves without his mercy."*

"Have it your own way," said HYPOCRISY, who then turned to FORMALIST to talk about the test match.

The path began to head upwards, and the travellers did not talk much together, but occasionally the two Vain-Glories would goad CHRISTIAN with cryptic comments about *laws and ordinances.* It was clear they thought that they were just as conscientious as CHRISTIAN.

"I don't know why he thinks he's superior to us," said FORMALIST. "Where did he get those clothes for a start – Oxfam?" They made curious noises that would probably be called sniggering.

*"By laws and ordinances you will not be saved,"* said CHRISTIAN, "*since you came not in by the door.* If you want to know, my clothes were given to me by the Lord of the place to which I am going. I look at them as an evidence of his kindness to me, because the jeans and tee-short I set out in were in a poor state after all the difficulties I encountered.

"When I reach the gate of the city, the Lord will recognise me. Not only am I wearing the clothes he gave me, but I also have a mark on my forehead – perhaps you haven't noticed?"

The other two peered at his forehead and suppressed a laugh.

"That was given me at the foot of the cross, *in the day that my burden fell off my shoulders,*" CHRISTIAN went on. "Not only that, I have this Roll, to give in at the Celestial Gate. I notice that you two have no special clothes, no mark and no Roll, since you did not come through the proper gate."

FORMALIST flicked an invisible speck of dirt off the lapel of his impeccable suit. "Not special enough?" he said smugly. "I'll have you know this is the best money can buy."

He and HYPOCRISY gave a yell of laughter, and from then on they simply ignored CHRISTIAN, who kept his spirits up by reading from his Roll.

After a while they came to the foot of a hill. A sign at the bottom said, 'Difficulty Hill - Gradient 1:3'. The road now split into three: one track went off to the left, one to the right, but the narrow way led straight up the hill.

It looked like a stiff climb. CHRISTIAN took a drink from a spring beside the road, and then started up the hill, singing to himself for encouragement. Thinking back to the last Prom Praise, he sang of his confidence that the road up Difficulty was the way to life:

*"The hill, though high, I covet to ascend,*
*The difficulty will not me offend.*
*For I perceive the way to life lies here;*
*Come, pluck up, heart, let's neither faint nor fear.*
*Better, tho' difficult, the right way to go,*
*Than wrong, though easy, where the end is woe."*

FORMALIST and HYPOCRISY stopped when they saw how steep the hill was. "We needn't bother going that way," said HYPOCHRISY. "I bet these other roads simply skirt the hill and meet up on the other side. There's no point in wearing ourselves out like that idiot – let's take the low roads." They agreed.

FORMALIST took the right hand path, which happened to be called Danger Lane, and which led him into a thick forest, while HYPOCRISY turned left into Destruction Road. This took him into a region *full of dark mountains, where he stumbled and fell, and rose no more.*

CHRISTIAN started up the hill at a cracking pace, but soon slowed down, and eventually was reduced to clambering on his hands and knees.

He was very grateful to see, halfway up the hill, a little garden, *made by the Lord of the Hill, for the refreshing of weary travellers.*

CHRISTIAN sat down on a bench among the greenery and pulled out his Roll to read. He began to admire his new clothes and eventually, feeling relaxed and thankful, he drifted off to sleep.

The Roll fell from his hand, and landed under the bench.

CHRISTIAN woke with a start to find that the daylight was already fading. In his dream he had heard someone quoting Proverbs 6:6: **'Look to the ant, thou sluggard! Consider her ways and be wise'**, and he leapt to his feet and charged up the hill to the top.

As he came over the brow of the hill, he saw two men running towards him.

They were dressed in camouflage gear, wearing heavy boots and stab vests. One of them, carrying a backpack with first aid equipment, was TIMOROUS, while the other, who appeared to be carrying a flare gun, was called MISTRUST.

"Hey stop!" called CHRISTIAN. "What's wrong? You're running the wrong way. The City of Zion is that way."

"We know," said TIMOROUS. "We thought this hill was difficult enough, but I'm not kidding, it's a jungle up there. Danger on every side. It's not worth it, mate. We've turned back."

"Take it from me," said MISTRUST, who had a South African accent, "it's seriously hazardous. We encountered a couple of lions on the path back there; trust me, I know about lions. I've seen what they can do to their prey. It would have been madness to go any further."

CHRISTIAN stared at the two of them as they ran off.

"Now I'm afraid to go on," he said, "But what other options do I have? Where can I be safe? If I can get to the Celestial City, I'm sure I will be secure there."

He told himself he must press on. "*To go back is nothing but death; to go forward is fear of death,"* he thought, but beyond that fear would be life everlasting. *"I will yet go forward!"*

MISTRUST and TIMOROUS were slipping and sliding back down into the valley, but CHRISTIAN continued onwards up the hill.

However, he felt nervous and reached into his inside pocket for the Roll of parchment, which he found comforting to read.

To his horror, it was not there.

# 10 THE PALACE BEAUTIFUL

He stopped and searched all his pockets. Where could he have lost it? Where did he have it last? It came to him: the little garden halfway up the hill! He must have dropped the Roll of parchment when he fell asleep on the bench.

*Falling down upon his knees, he asked God forgiveness*, and then retraced his steps to look for the Roll. Tears came into his eyes when he thought about losing the precious document, and he blamed himself for being so stupid as to fall asleep, when he should only have paused for a little rest.

He walked back along the path, looking on either side, searching under bushes. When he came to the garden, he smacked his head in frustration and anger at himself: *"Oh, wretched man that I am, that I should sleep in the daytime! That I should sleep in the midst of difficulty!... How many steps have I took in vain! (thus it happened to Israel; for their sin they were sent back again by the way of the Red Sea); and I am made to tread those steps with sorrow, which I might have trod with delight."*

He realised he was going to have to walk this leg of the journey three times, when he need only have done it once, and that it would soon be nightfall.

He paced the little garden but there was no sign of his Roll. He went down on his knees by the bench to pray for forgiveness and strength, and when he opened his eyes he saw, through the slats of the bench, his Roll of parchment!

*Who can tell how joyful this man was when he had gotten his Roll again! For this Roll was the assurance of his life and acceptance at the desired haven.*

Putting it securely in the inside pocket of his jacket, he thanked God for showing him where it was and started back up the hill.

As he came over the top of the hill, the sun fell below the horizon, and he kicked himself again for wasting daylight hours in sleep. He shivered as he thought of the possibility of lions ahead, prowling for prey in the dark.

He walked warily on in the gathering dusk. As he came over a ridge he saw in front of him what looked like a large stately home, set in a park. A sign said this was the Palace Beautiful, and the road ran beside it.

*So I saw in my dream that he made haste and went forward, that if possible he might get lodging there.* There was a very narrow passage from the road to the porter's lodge; and seated in the passage were two lions.

Now he could see what had spooked MISTRUST and TIMOROUS. As he hesitated, he heard a shout from the Porter at the lodge, whose name was WATCHFUL: *"Is thy faith so small?* Don't be scared of the lions - they are chained up. They're just to test your faith, and to expose those who have no faith. Keep in the middle of the path and you'll come to no harm."

CHRISTIAN took a deep breath and walked forward with his heart in his mouth. He walked carefully and slowly down the middle of the path, constantly looking from side to side to check he was equidistant from each wall. The lions roared and strained at their chains as he passed them, but they did him no harm.

Once past them, he clapped his hands in a burst of relief and almost danced up to the porter's lodge.

"They're just pussycats really," said the porter, throwing the beasts a couple of chunks of bleeding meat. They settled down to eat contentedly.

"Is this a National Trust property, or can I stay here for the night?" asked CHRISTIAN.

*"This house was built by the Lord of the hill; and he built it for the relief and security of pilgrims,"* said WATCHFUL. "But who are you, and where are you headed?"

*"I am come from the City of Destruction, and I am going to Mount Zion,"* said CHRISTIAN. *"My name is now CHRISTIAN; but my name at the first was GRACELESS: I came of the race of Japhet, whom God will persuade to dwell in the tents of Shem."*

"You've left it a bit late to find a bed for the night, haven't you?"

"I am sorry to say I fell asleep and lost the Roll I was given to present at the Celestial City as evidence that I may enter. I went over the hill and then realised I hadn't got it, so I went back up the hill and down the other side to look for it and couldn't find it and then I found it so I had to go back up the hill where I'd already come and down the other side and now I'm here."

"Righto, get your breath back," said WATCHFUL. "Well, I'll tell you what I'll do. I'll call one of the sisters here and if she likes what you have to say, she will *bring you in to the rest of the family, according to the rules of the house."*

WATCHFUL picked up the phone and spoke to someone, and shortly afterwards a nun appeared. She had an extraordinarily beautiful face, and her name was DISCRETION.

The nun smiled at CHRISTIAN and invited him to follow her. She led him from the lodge across the gravelled driveway and up several steps to the main entrance.

The outer door opened into a domed lobby which was dominated by a large portrait of a Lady Richeldis. Passing through a pair of stained glass double doors they entered an enormous galleried entrance hall, with a wide marble staircase rising to the first floor.

DISCRETION led CHRISTIAN to a seating area around an elaborate fireplace.

“So, tell me about your journey,” she said.

CHRISTIAN told her his story, and it was only at the end that she asked him his name. “My name is CHRISTIAN,” he said, “and I would really like to spend the night here, if that would be possible.”

# 11 PIETY, PRUDENCE & CHARITY

She smiled, but there were tears in her eyes. After a little pause she said, "Let me call a few more of the family." She went to the door and CHRISTIAN heard her call in her gentle voice.

Three more nuns joined them and she introduced them as PRUDENCE, PIETY, and CHARITY. They chatted a while and then the nuns said he would be welcome to stay. They offered him a beer and, while supper was being prepared, they sat round the fire and the nuns asked CHRISTIAN about his experiences.

PIETY wanted to know why CHRISTIAN had started on his journey: "*I was driven out,*" he said, "*by a dreadful sound that was in mine ears: to wit, that unavoidable destruction did attend me if* I stayed there."

He told her how he had met EVANGELIST and how he had eventually found the wicket gate. "I had no idea what to do," he confessed. "If I hadn't met EVANGELIST I would never have found the gate."

PIETY asked if he had visited the INTERPRETER.

*"Yes,"* said CHRISTIAN, "*and did see such things there, the remembrance of which will stick by me as long as I live.*"

Three things in particular had made a deep impression on him, he realised: *how Christ in despite of Satan, maintains his work of grace in the heart;* the despair of the man in the iron cage, who had sinned so much that he had lost all hope of God's mercy; and the dream of the man who saw the Day of Judgment in his sleep.

"Oh yes, the film," said PIETY. "What did you think of the dream?"

"It was very disturbing," said CHRISTIAN. *"It made my heart ache as he was telling of it; but yet I am glad I heard it."*

He told her how the INTERPRETER also showed him the stately palace occupied by people dressed in gold. "I was thinking how mean the guards looked when this amazingly brave guy came up and cut his way right through them. It was really exciting. He was invited to come in and win eternal glory – good for him. I found it all fascinating, and could have stayed for hours, but I knew I had to get on with the journey."

"And what else did you see on the way?" asked PIETY.

*"Saw!"* exclaimed CHRISTIAN. *"Why I went but a little farther, and I saw One, as I thought in my mind, hang bleeding upon the tree, and the very sight of him made the burden fall off my back (for I groaned under a weary burden)."*

He thought about the extraordinary experience he had had there, as he stood under the cross. "Three *shining ones* came up to me – one testified that my sins were forgiven, one stripped me of my worn-out clothes and gave me a complete new outfit, and one set this mark on my forehead and gave me a Roll of parchment."

CHRISTIAN reached into his pocket and brought it out.

*"But you saw more than this, did you not?"* asked PIETY.

"These were the best things, but there were other incidents I remember," he said, and he told her about SIMPLE, SLOTH, and PRESUMPTION, and his attempts to waken them. He told her about FORMALIST and HYPOCRISY, who claimed to be going to Zion but who had cheated by climbing over a wall to get on to the road.

"They took the wrong path and are lost – I did tell them but they didn't listen to me," he added.

"Climbing the hill was very hard for me, but so was walking past those lions. To be honest, if that good man, the porter, had not been so helpful, I might have made the mistake of turning back at that point. *But I thank God I am here, and I thank you for receiving me."*

DISCRETION poured another beer into his glass, and at this point PRUDENCE asked a question. She had a slight Scottish accent. *"Do you not think sometimes of the country from whence you came?"* she asked.

"Sometimes," replied CHRISTIAN, "But looking back now, I can't stand the place. If I had better feelings about it I might miss it, *but now I desire a better country, that is, an heavenly."*

"Do you still carry with you some reminders of home?" asked PRUDENCE.

"Yes," replied CHRISTIAN, "but I wish I didn't. I still carry with me those superficial, materialistic desires that I used to revel in. Like everyone else in the place where I lived, money, sex, food and possessions were all we ever thought of. Now I despise that way of thinking and, if I could, I would be free of it. But even though I'm trying to be a better person, that old thinking is still with me."

"But there are times, aren't there, when you are free of bad thoughts?" asked PRUDENCE.

“Yes, but they don’t happen often,” said CHRISTIAN. “When they do, *they are to me golden hours.”* He looked across at the television in the corner: the picture was on, showing the news, but the sound was off.

“What do you do to keep your thoughts in check?” asked PRUDENCE.

“*When I think of what I saw at the cross, that will do it,”* said CHRISTIAN. “When I look at my new clothes, when I look at the Roll I’m carrying, *and when my thoughts wax warm about whither I am going.* That all works for me.”

“So what really drives you to press on with your journey to Mount Zion?”

CHRISTIAN thought for a minute. “I think because there I hope to see alive my Saviour who hung dead on the cross,” he said. “There I hope to be rid of all the selfish desires that persist in me. At Mount Zion there is no death and I shall be with all the others who seek what I seek. *For to tell you truth, I love him because I was by him eased of my burden, and I am weary of my inward sickness; I would fain be where I shall die no more, and with the company that shall continually cry, ‘Holy, holy, holy’.”*

CHARITY was one of the older nuns, and she now asked: “*Have you a family? Are you a married man?"*

CHRISTIAN looked at her and wondered why she asked. Did she regret the cost of her vocation, and the lost opportunity to have children of her own? He said as gently as he could*: “I have a wife and four small children.”*

“*And why did you not bring them along with you?”* asked CHARITY.

Tears filled CHRISTIAN's eyes, and he said, "Oh, I wanted to. But they were all completely opposed to my pilgrimage."

"But why didn't you warn them of the danger of being left behind?" asked CHARITY.

"Believe me I did, I really did," said CHRISTIAN, "but they thought I was joking, I suppose. They didn't believe me."

"But did you really pray about this?" CHARITY pressed him.

"Yes," said CHRISTIAN, miserably, "with all my heart. I do love my wife and poor children."

"And did you tell them what was bothering you, and your fear that you were all heading for ruin?"

"Of course, over and over again," said CHRISTIAN. "It must have been obvious from the way I looked, from my distress, because I was so afraid of the judgment hanging over us. But it wasn't enough to persuade them to come with me."

"So what was their excuse for not coming with you?" asked CHARITY.

"Well, sweet CHARITY," said CHRISTIAN, "my wife was a real big spender. She couldn't think of giving up her shopping and her John Lewis card, and the kids wouldn't be parted from their Nintendos and Play Stations and mobile phones, so they let me go off alone."

"Do you think, perhaps, they did not come with you because they thought you were a hypocrite?"

"I know that I often failed to live up to the things I believed," replied CHRISTIAN. "Yet I really was careful not to do anything that would make them averse to going on pilgrimage with me.

They would sometimes criticise me for refusing to join in things that they thought were harmless.

"So, if you want to know the real reason why they would not come with me, I can only think it was my reluctance to sin against God or to wrong my neighbour in any way."

CHARITY nodded. "Remember Cain," she said. "He hated his brother Abel because it was Abel who was a good person. If your family didn't like your behaviour*, they thereby show themselves to be implacable to good.* You have delivered your soul from their bad influence."

In my dream I saw that supper was now ready, and CHRISTIAN and the nuns sat down to eat together. The food and wine were excellent, and their conversation was all about the Lord of the Hill, what he had done, and why, and his reasons for building the house.

# 12 ABOUT THE LORD OF THE HILL

From their conversation, I heard that the Lord of the Hill had been *a great warrior, and had fought with and slain him that had the power of death; but not without great danger to himself, which made me love him the more.*

The nuns told CHRISTIAN that the battle had cost the Lord a lot of blood*; but he did it out of pure love for his country.* Some of the nuns affirmed that the Lord was alive and they had seen him and talked with him after his death on the cross.

They had heard from his own lips of his great love for poor pilgrims like CHRISTIAN, so great that he had stripped himself of his high position in order to help the poor, and had vowed not to dwell at Mount Zion alone. He had made pilgrims princes, even though *they were beggars born, and their original had been the dunghill.* And so they chatted until midnight.

After singing the Walsingham Pilgrim Hymn, they said a prayer together for their Lord's protection, and then all went to bed.

They gave CHRISTIAN a large bedroom looking east, so that he could see the sunrise; the name on the door of the room was 'Peace', *where he slept till break of day; and then he awoke and sang:*

*"Where am I now? Is this the love and care*
*Of Jesus for the men that pilgrims are,*

*Thus to provide? That I should be forgiven!*
*And dwell already the next door to heaven!"*

After breakfast, the nuns urged him not to continue his journey until he had seen some of the treasures in the house.

They took him first into the Library, where there were ancient records of the genealogy of the Lord of the Hill, *that he was the Son of the Ancient of Days, and came by that eternal generation.* There were reports of all that the Lord had done, the names of the hundreds of people he had taken into his service and accounts of how he would provide for them for ever.

They showed him shelves full of books about the lives of some of the Lord's servants and all they had done: some had *"subdued kingdoms, wrought righteousness, obtained promises, stopped the mouths of lions, quenched the violence of fire, escaped the edge of the sword; out of weakness were made strong, waxed valiant in fight, and turned to flight the armies of the Aliens".*

CHRISTIAN found the shelves with the house journals, which showed how generous the Lord had been, even to people who had in the past insulted or abused him. There were files of correspondence, current and from times long past, together with predictions of things that had come true, to the delight of the pilgrims and the confounding of their enemies.

All that day CHRISTIAN read in the Library, and the following day they took him into the Armoury, which was housed in a large barn behind the main house. It was stocked with all sorts of equipment that the Lord had provided for pilgrims: *sword, shield, helmet, breastplate, All Prayer, and shoes that would not wear out.* The stocks were endless – enough to equip as many pilgrims for the service of their Lord as there are stars in the sky.

In the afternoon, the nuns showed him what they called their Cabinet of Wonders, in a long gallery on the first floor. On display were astonishing artefacts from the Old Testament: *Moses' rod; the hammer and nail with which Jael slew Sisera; the pitchers, trumpets, and lamps too, with which Gideon put to flight the armies of Midian.*

There was the ox-goad with which Shamgar killed 600 men, the jawbone with which Samson performed mighty feats of strength and the sling with which David killed Goliath. There, too, was the sword *with which their Lord will kill the man of sin, in the day that he shall rise up to the prey.* CHRISTIAN was amazed at the display, and spent all afternoon walking around and studying the items.

The next day, the nuns asked him to remain for one more day. Tomorrow was forecast to be a fine day, they told him. One of the nuns told him that on a clear day you could see forever – and she could point out to him the Delectable Mountains. This would encourage him, she suggested, as he would know that when he reached the mountains he would be much nearer his destination.

So CHRISTIAN spent one more night, and after breakfast they all went to the top of the house and looked south. And there at a great distance *he saw a most pleasant mountainous country, beautified with woods, vineyards, fruits of all sorts; flowers also, with springs and fountains, very delectable to behold.*

"What is that place called?" asked CHRISTIAN.

"It is known as *Immanuel's Land,"* they told him, "and just like this house, it is a place for all pilgrims. When you get there, the Shepherds will point out to you the gate of the Celestial City."

"Time for me to move on," said CHRISTIAN again, and this time the nuns agreed. They took him back to the Armoury, and kitted him out from head to foot with waterproofs and protective gear, in case he should encounter trouble along the way.

At the gate, CHRISTIAN asked WATCHFUL, the porter, if he had seen any other pilgrims pass by.

"Indeed," said WATCHFUL, "there is a man ahead of you. He told me his name was FAITHFUL."

"Good heavens," said CHRISTIAN, "I know him – he is the only reliable plumber in town! He lives just down the road from me! Is he far ahead?"

"He should be at the bottom of the hill by now," WATCHFUL replied.

*"Well," said CHRISTIAN, "good porter, the Lord be with thee, and add to all thy blessings much increase for the kindness that thou hast showed to me."*

DISCRETION, PIETY, CHARITY, and PRUDENCE said they would accompany him to the foot of the hill. They walked along, chatting, until the road began to descend. As he looked down into the valley, CHRISTIAN said, "I thought it was hard work coming up the hill, but it looks just as dangerous going down."

"You're right," said PRUDENCE. "It is not easy for a man to go down into the Valley of Humiliation without taking a tumble. That is why we will accompany you to the bottom of the hill."

So he picked his way down, warily, but even so his foot slipped now and then.

Then in my dream I saw that when they reached the bottom of the hill, the kind nuns gave CHRISTIAN a picnic bag containing *a loaf of bread, a bottle of wine, and a cluster of raisins.* And so they parted, and CHRISTIAN went on his way.

As he set off through the Valley of Humiliation, poor CHRISTIAN found the going tough.

# 13 APOLLYON

After the encouragement and fellowship he had enjoyed with the nuns, he was now on his own, and he began to feel low.

His thoughts troubled him; he seemed to hear voices in his head mocking him. "What's the point?" they said. "You'll never complete this pilgrimage. You've barely managed to get this far. Who do you think you are?"

He wondered if he should turn around and go back, or carry on, ignoring the negative voices. But as he thought further, he realised that if he tried to repress these feelings, they would still always be with him, ready to come out at a time of weakness. He needed to confront them now and face them down.

So as he walked on, he delved into his deepest feelings and motivations. The more he analysed, the uglier he found the prospect.

As a child, inspired by the film of 'Pete's Dragon', he had created an imaginary dragon friend called Puff during a seaside holiday in Honalee. This had given him comfort in times of loneliness and uncertainty; talking to Puff had enabled him to cope with the fears and confusion of growing up. On reaching adolescence, Puff had sort of faded away, a bit like Pete's Dragon in the film.

This time, as he tried to recall Puff to talk to him, the picture in his mind did not look anything like Pete's Dragon. Instead, a monster took shape, *hideous to behold; he was clothed with scales like a fish (and they are his pride); he had wings like a dragon; feet like a bear; and out of his belly came fire and smoke; and his mouth was as the mouth of a lion.*

This is no Puff, this is APOLLYON, the destroyer, thought CHRISTIAN, remembering his schoolboy Greek. And there in front of him, on the road, appeared APOLLYON himself.

The monster came close and stared at CHRISTIAN contemptuously. "What are you doing here?" asked APOLLYON. His voice was as smooth as his skin was scaly.

*"I am come from the City of Destruction,"* replied CHRISTIAN, "*which is the place of all evil, and am going to the City of Zion."*

"I see," said APOLLYON, "so you are one of my subjects running away. The City of Destruction is mine. I am the prince and god of it. Why are you running away from your King? If I did not think you could be of further use to me, I would knock you to the ground here and now."

CHRISTIAN resisted. "I was indeed born in your world. But being one of your subjects was hard and a man could not live on the wages you paid, *for the wages of sin is death.* When I came to realise this, I did what any prudent person would do, and looked for a way out."

"No king likes to lose a subject and I don't want to lose you," said APOLLYON. He adopted a friendly tone. "If you don't like the wages and conditions, come back and I promise to improve your terms."

"I can't do that," said CHRISTIAN. "I have sworn allegiance to the King of Kings, so in fairness, how can I go back to your service?"

APOLLYON laughed. "You have leapt out of the frying pan into the fire," he said smugly. "But I usually find people like you lose their enthusiasm for being in his service, after a while, and they come back to me. You can easily do the same, and all will be well."

"But I have promised to be his faithful soldier and servant for the rest of my life," said CHRISTIAN. "How can I go back on this and not be punished as a traitor?"

"You turned traitor on me," APOLLYON pointed out. "However, I am willing to forgive and forget if you return."

"I swore allegiance to you before I woke up to the realities of your rule," responded CHRISTIAN. "Anyway, I believe that my new King is able to forgive me for all that I did for you in the past. And in all honesty, destructive APOLLYON, I actually prefer *his servants, his government, his company, and country, better than thine.* So push off."

APOLLYON sighed and put on a voice of sweet reason. "Think rationally about what lies ahead. You know that most of your King's servants come to a sticky end, because they go against me. How many of them have met terrible deaths? And if you think his service is better than mine, how come he never stirs himself to rescue his people from me? But all the world knows how often I take back from him, *by power or fraud,* those who faithfully serve me. I can deliver you, too, from this King of yours."

"The reason he doesn't rescue them, *is on purpose to try their love, whether they will cleave to him to the end,"* CHRISTIAN said. He paused, and then continued. "As for the sticky end, on the contrary, it is a glorious end. Followers of my King do not expect deliverance, but look forward to the coming of the Kingdom in all its fullness, and the glory of the King."

"You have already proved yourself disloyal to your King. How do you think he will reward you?" asked APOLLYON, slyly. "You almost collapsed in the Slough of Despond, you tried all sorts of wrong ways to get rid of your burden, you went to sleep and lost your Roll, you were nearly scared off by the lions, and when you talk of your journey, it is clear you are doing it for your own glory and self-satisfaction."

"All you say is true," admitted CHRISTIAN, "and there are many other things you have left off your list. But the King *whom I serve and honour is merciful and ready to forgive*. It was my upbringing in your country that gave me these shortcomings and I have *groaned under them, being sorry for them, and have obtained pardon of my Prince."*

At this, APOLLYON went berserk. "I hate your King!" he raged, "I hate him, his laws and his people. I hate you and I'm here to stop you going any further on your journey!"

"Be careful," said CHRISTIAN, calmly, "*I am in the King's highway, the way of holiness:* you need to watch out."

"Don't you lecture me," shrieked APOLLYON, "I am not afraid of you! Prepare to die!"

With this he started to bombard CHRISTIAN with accusations and temptations like flaming darts, but CHRISTIAN held up his faith like a shield. He realised he needed to go on the attack, and so he pulled out his sword.

APOLLYON was throwing darts as thick as hail. He wounded CHRISTIAN in his head, his hand and his foot. CHRISTIAN felt as if his understanding of why he was on this road, his faith and his resolve, had all been weakened. He staggered back and APOLLYON redoubled his attack.

*CHRISTIAN again took courage, and resisted as manfully as he could. This sore combat lasted for above half a day, even till CHRISTIAN was almost quite spent. For you must know that*

*CHRISTIAN, by reason of his wounds, must needs grow weaker and weaker.*

APOLLYON saw his opportunity, and began to close in on CHRISTIAN. The monster grabbed him by the shoulders and they wrestled fiercely until APOLLYON threw CHRISTIAN to the ground. As he fell, his sword flew out of his hand.

"I have you now!" cried APOLLYON triumphantly, and CHRISTIAN thought his end had come. But as the monster raised his arms for the final blow, CHRISTIAN reached out for his sword lying on the road beside him and thrust it into the scaly body, quoting from Micah 7:8 in his Book: **"Rejoice not over me, O mine enemy; when I fall, I shall arise."**

APOLLYON fell back, as though he had received a mortal wound. Seeing this, CHRISTIAN attacked again quoting Romans 8:37: **"Nay, in all these things we are more than conquerors through Him that loved us."**

With a roar, APOLLYON spread his dragon's wings and flew away.

If you had not watched this battle as I did, you cannot imagine the ugliness and fury of APOLLYON, nor CHRISTIAN's anguish. He battled all the time with a look of grim determination on his face, only giving a smile when he saw he had wounded the monster with his two-edged sword.

When the battle was over, CHRISTIAN knelt down to give thanks for his deliverance. Sitting beside the road for some rest, he wrote a song, setting it to a Taizé chant:

*Great Beelzebub, the captain of this fiend,*
*Designed my ruin; therefore to this end*
*He sent him harnessed out, and he with rage*
*That hellish was, did fiercely me engage.*

*But blessed Michael helped me, and I,*
*By dint of sword did quickly make him fly:*
*Therefore to him let me give lasting praise*
*And thanks, and bless his holy name always!*

Then, out of nowhere, a hand appeared, holding out to him some leaves. They were leaves from the tree of life and when CHRISTIAN rubbed them on his wounds, his cuts and bruises healed immediately.

He took out the food and drink the nuns had given him, and when he was refreshed, he set off again on his journey. He was on his guard now for adversaries, but APOLLYON did not reappear and he made his way through the valley without meeting anyone else.

At the end of the Valley of Humiliation was another valley, called the Valley of the Shadow of Death. CHRISTIAN had to walk through this too, following the road to the Celestial City.

The valley was lonely and desolate; *the prophet Jeremiah thus describes it: "A wilderness, a land of deserts and of pits, a land of drought, and of the shadow of death; a land that no man (but a Christian) passeth through, and where no man dwelt."*

For CHRISTIAN, this place brought an even worse experience than his fight with APOLLYON.

# 14 THE VALLEY OF THE SHADOW OF DEATH

As CHRISTIAN began to descend into the Shadow of Death, he met two men who reminded him of the ten spies in Numbers 13 who could only find fault with the Promised Land.

"Hello," CHRISTIAN greeted them. "Where are you going?"

"Back!" they said, "We're going back, and so will you if you value your life or your sanity."

"Why, what is the matter?"

"Matter?" they retorted, "We'll tell you what's the matter. We went as far as we dared, and if we'd gone any further we wouldn't be here now to warn you. We were almost in the Valley of the Shadow of Death! But luckily we saw the danger before we reached it."

"But what did you see?" asked CHRISTIAN.

"See?" they shrieked. *"Why the valley itself, which is as dark as pitch. We also saw here the hobgoblins, satyrs, and dragons of the pit; we heard also in that valley a continual howling and yelling, as of a people under unutterable misery, who were sat down in affliction and irons: and over that valley hangs the discouraging clouds of confusion. Death also doth always spread his wings over it. In a word, it is every whit dreadful; being utterly without order."*

Admittedly, this did not sound good. "However, this is the way I have to go to get to my journey's end," CHRISTIAN insisted.

"Have it your own way," they replied, "but it is not for us."

And the men walked back up the hill as CHRISTIAN continued his descent into the valley, on guard against any attack.

I saw in my dream, that as the road went further down the valley, there was a very deep ditch on the right hand side. Through the ages the blind have led the blind into this ditch, and both have perished.

On the left hand side there was a dangerous bog, so deep that even a good man could find no bottom for his foot to stand upon. It was into this bog that King David once fell, and he would have been smothered, if God had not pulled him out. David wrote about this experience in Psalm 69.

The path was very narrow, and in the darkness CHRISTIAN struggled to avoid falling into the ditch on one side, or blundering into the bog on the other. I heard him sighing bitterly as he groped his way through the darkness, unable to see where to put his feet.

In the dream I could see that in the middle of this valley was the mouth of hell, standing close to the path. "What can I do?" thought CHRISTIAN. Every so often flame and smoke would belch out, with a hideous noise. Unlike APOLLYON, these were not adversaries that feared a sword. CHRISTIAN saw that he needed some other defence, and so he turned to *another weapon, called 'All Prayer'.*

I heard him cry out the words of Psalm 116:4 - **"O LORD, I beseech Thee, deliver my soul!"**

So CHRISTIAN travelled on, dodging the bursts of flame, and scared out of his wits. All around him was such a clamour and din that he feared he was going to be torn to pieces or trodden underfoot in some monstrous mêlée.

This went on mile after mile, until at one point he thought he was about to be attacked by a gang of demons. He stopped and came close to turning back. But then he thought he might already be more than halfway through the valley, and he remembered what he had already endured. Going back might be worse than going forward, so he decided to press on.

*Yet the fiends seemed to come nearer and nearer;* but just as they seemed to be upon him, he cried out in a strong voice: *"I will walk in the strength of the Lord God;" so they gave back, and came no farther.*

I now noticed something strange: poor CHRISTIAN was so confused that he could not recognise his own voice. I saw as he came near the mouth of the burning pit that *one of the wicked ones got behind him,* and whispered in his ear some terrible blasphemies.

CHRISTIAN took these thoughts to be his own, and this put him into a state of panic and guilt: he could not understand how he could blaspheme against the Lord he loved so much!

He felt he could not possibly have such thoughts, but he was too distressed either to cover his ears, or to realise from where the blasphemies really came.

CHRISTIAN had struggled on for hours in this abject condition, when he thought he heard a voice ahead of him chanting the words of Psalm 23: **"Yea, though I walk through the valley**

**of the shadow of death, I will fear no evil; for Thou art with me; Thy rod and Thy staff, they comfort me."**

This cheered him up, for three reasons:

Firstly, he discovered he was not the only person in this valley who trusted in God.

Secondly, he thought that if God was with others in this terrible place, then God would also be with him, even if he couldn't *perceive* it right now, because of the darkness and terrors.

Thirdly, if he could catch up with the person ahead, he would have company on his journey.

So he walked on, calling out to the other traveller. But there was no reply, because the man ahead of him thought he was alone in the valley.

Eventually, the day broke. *Then said CHRISTIAN*, quoting Amos 5:8: "He **turneth the shadow of death into the morning**."

In the early light of the dawn he looked back, not from a desire to retrace his steps, but to see what he had just been through. He could now see more clearly the ditch and the bog, and how narrow was the path between them.

He also spotted *the hobgoblins, and satyrs, and dragons of the pit,* but they were all distant now, because they would not approach him in daylight. CHRISTIAN thought of the words of Job in his Book: **"He discovereth deep things out of darkness, and bringeth out to light the shadow of death."**

I saw that CHRISTIAN was quite moved by his deliverance from the dangers in the valley. Although he had been afraid when he entered the valley, looking back in the light he could see the risks more clearly, and realised far more profoundly what he had been through.

The rising of the sun was another mercy to CHRISTIAN because, although the first part of the Valley of the Shadow of Death was dangerous, the second part, into which he was now heading, was even more hazardous.

As he looked down the valley in the morning light he could see that the path was *set so full of snares, traps, gins and nets here, and so full of pits, pitfalls, deep holes and shelvings down there,* that had it been dark he would have stood no chance of getting through unscathed.

But the sun was up, and he again thought of the lament of Job, remembering past times: **"His candle shone upon my head, and when by His light I walked through darkness."**

Walking now under clear blue skies, he came to the end of the valley.

Now in my dream I saw that CHRISTIAN was walking through a large clearing in the bush where human remains were scattered randomly in the dust: *blood, bones, ashes, and mingled bodies of men, even of pilgrims that had gone this way formerly.*

While I looked around this macabre landscape, wondering how these travellers had perished, I noticed a cave in the hillside where two giants, POPE and PAGAN had lived in times gone by. It was through their power and tyranny that these men had been cruelly put to death.

Yet CHRISTIAN walked past this place unhindered, which surprised me. However, I have since learned that PAGAN had been dead a long time.

As for the other, though he is still alive, he is so old and decrepit *that he can now do little more than sit in his cave's mouth grinning at pilgrims as they go by, and biting his nails, because he cannot come at them.*

As CHRISTIAN passed the cave he hesitated, not knowing what to think, when the old man muttered at him: *"You will never mend, till more of you be burned."*

But the man was clearly incapable of hurting him, so CHRISTIAN ignored him and, looking forward with hope, he walked on by and came to no harm.

For some reason CHRISTIAN started humming the *Dies Irae* from Verdi's *Requiem.* He always remembered the performance at school when the headmaster had led the trombones off to disaster, and it brought a smile to his face even now.

He started to put together some words and imagined an orgy of brass instruments in an orchestral accompaniment:

*O world of wonders! (I can say no less)*
*That I should be preserv'd in that distress*
*That I have met with here! O blessed be*
*That hand that from it hath deliver'd me!*
*Dangers in darkness, Devils, Hell and Sin,*
*Did compass me while I this Vale was in.*
*Yea Snares & Pits, & Traps & Nets did lie*
*My path about, that worthless silly I*
*Might have been catch't entangled, and cast down:*
*But since I live, Let JESUS wear the Crown.*

# 15 FAITHFUL'S STORY

Now as CHRISTIAN went on his way, the path climbed up to a grassy hillock from which pilgrims could see the way ahead. From there, he could at last see FAITHFUL, further along the road. "Hey!" he yelled. "Ahoy there, FAITHFUL, wait for me!"

But FAITHFUL shouted back, *"No, I am upon my life; and the Avenger of Blood is behind me!"* So CHRISTIAN raced down the path and managed to overtake his friend. "The last shall be first," he thought and, feeling very pleased with himself at this burst of speed, he turned round, grinning, and promptly fell over.

FAITHFUL laughed and pulled him to his feet, and I saw them walk on together, having *sweet discourse of all things that had happened to them in their pilgrimage.*

"It is wonderful to see you again," said CHRISTIAN, "and it's great to have your company on this pleasant part of the journey."

"I had hoped to accompany you from the town," said FAITHFUL, "but you started out sooner than I expected. So I've had to do the journey this far on my own."

"How long did you stay in the City of Destruction before you set out after me?"

"Until I could stand it no longer," replied FAITHFUL. "There was a lot of talk that our city would be struck with fire and brimstone and burned to the ground, but I don't think people really believed it would happen. So everyone stayed put. I heard people laughing about your 'desperate journey', as they called it, but I thought you were right, and I made my escape too."

"What happened to PLIABLE?" asked CHRISTIAN.

"I heard he went off with you and fell in some kind of bog, but he won't talk about it. I heard he came back filthy and covered with mud, and stank like a bad drain. He's a laughing stock now and he finds it difficult to get work. He is far worse off than if he had never started on the journey."

"But why do people despise him, if they also despise the journey he gave up?"

"Oh, they think he's a hypocrite and a quitter, who hasn't the guts to stick with what he says he believes in," replied FAITHFUL. *"I think God has stirred up even his enemies to hiss at him, and make him a Proverb, because he hath forsaken the way.* I met him once in the street, but he crossed over to the other side of the road, obviously ashamed to talk about what had happened."

"I am really sorry to hear that," said CHRISTIAN. "I had high hopes for that man when we set off. Sadly it is a case of 2 Peter 2:22: **"The dog turns to his own vomit again," and, "the sow that was washed, to her wallowing in the mire."**
I fear he will perish along with the city."

"My fears entirely; *but who can hinder that which will be?"*

"Well, FAITHFUL, my old friend and plumber," said CHRISTIAN, "let's leave him. Tell me about your journey – I know you must have encountered some incredible things."

"I managed to avoid the Slough of Despond," FAITHFUL began, "and I arrived at the narrow gate, but was met there by a woman in a very low cut mini-dress who told me her name was WANTON. I thought of Joseph and Potiphar's wife, but she seemed intent on luring me off the path. She was very persuasive about the, er, delights in store for me, *promising me all manner of content."*

"I bet she did not *promise you the content of a good conscience*," joked CHRISTIAN.

"You know exactly what I mean," said FAITHFUL indignantly.

"You had a narrow escape, then."

"I am not sure I did entirely escape her," FAITHFUL muttered.

CHRISTIAN was aghast. "Don't tell me you had a romp in a haystack?"

"No, no, nothing like that," protested FAITHFUL, "I know all the warnings in Proverbs, but I had to shut my eyes and make a real effort to walk away. Anyway, I got a torrent of abuse from her when she saw I was determined to resist her charms."

"Hmm. Did anyone else have a go at you?"

"At the foot of Difficulty Hill I met this ancient chap, a decrepit old aristocrat, with whom I got into a long conversation about my pilgrimage. And would you believe it, he said, 'You look like an honest fellow – why don't you come and work for me?' I asked him who he was and where he lived, and he told me his name was Count Adam the First, and he lived in the Manor House by the Town of Deceit.

"Well, I asked him what this work was and how much he would pay me. *He told me that his work was many delights; and his wages, that I should be his heir at last.* Interesting, so I asked him more about his business and his other employees. *He told me that his house was maintained with all the dainties in the world; and that his Servants were those of his own begetting*. I asked him how many children he had, and he said he had no son, only daughters, who were called *The LUST of the FLESH, The LUST of the EYES, and The PRIDE of LIFE*, and I could marry all three if I wanted to."

"How bizarre," said CHRISTIAN.

"Indeed," replied FAITHFUL, "and he expected me to live with him until his death, which I guessed might not be very far away. I have to say it seemed a tempting offer, but then I spotted a coat of arms on his pocket watch, and I saw the motto *'Put off the old man with his deeds.'* I felt sure that in spite of his flattering words, as soon as I entered his house *he would sell me for a slave.*

"So I politely excused myself, and said I should be on my way. At that point he turned nasty and said he would send someone after me, who would *make my way bitter to my Soul.* I turned to go, but he grabbed my arm and yanked it so hard I thought he would pull it out of its socket. I yelled Romans 7:24: **"O wretched man that I am!"** and I got away and pressed on up the hill.

"About halfway up, I looked back and saw a man running towards me, really fast. As he got closer, I saw he was a Jewish Rabbi, in trainers. He pounded up the slope as if he was training for the Olympics. He overtook me where the bench stands."

"I know that place," said CHRISTIAN, excitedly. "That's where I fell asleep and lost my Roll."

"But listen to this: as soon as he reached me, the Rabbi punched me in the face and knocked me out. When I came to, I wiped the blood from my mouth and asked him why he had beaten me up. *He said, because of my secret inclining to Adam the First.* Then he punched me again, in the chest. I fell backwards and was out for the count again.

"This time when I came to, I cried out for mercy; but he said, *'I know not how to show mercy,' and with that knocked me down again.*

"As I sank into unconsciousness I thought this was the end."

# 16 MOSES THE MERCILESS

CHRISTIAN was horrified.

They were passing a farm shop which had tables and chairs outside, and CHRISTIAN pulled FAITHFUL towards it. His eye had been caught by the mention of carrot cake on a chalk board, so armed with coffee and cake, they sat at a table under an oak tree beside the road.

"Go on," said CHRISTIAN. "So why are you still alive?"

"He would have finished me off, without a doubt," said FAITHFUL, "if it had not been for a passer-by who told him to stop."

"Who was your rescuer?"

"I did not recognise him at first," said FAITHFUL, "but as he went by, I looked up through my tears and blood and saw the holes in his hands and in his side; *then I concluded that He was our Lord.* So I picked myself up and went on up the hill."

*"That man that overtook you was Moses,"* said CHRISTIAN. *"He spareth none.* He does not know how to show mercy to those who transgress his law."

"I know that now, and it was not the first time we have had a set-to. When I was living safely at home in the city, he *told me he would burn my house over my head, if I stayed there."*

"After you'd got up the hill, didn't you see the big house?" asked CHRISTIAN. "Why didn't you stop? Did the lions put you off?"

"I saw the house, and the lions. But they were actually asleep. It was only noon when I got there, and I wanted to press on, so I greeted the porter and went down the other side of the hill."

"He told me he saw you, but you should have called in. It was an astonishing place. Did you meet anybody in the Valley of Humility?"

"Huh," grunted FAITHFUL. "I met DISCONTENT – do you know him? A prominent member of his Parochial Church Council. He tried to persuade me to turn back, because he said the valley was *altogether without Honour.*

"He argued that if I went that way, I would upset all my friends, PRIDE, ARROGANCY, SELF-CONCEIT, WORLDLY-GLORY and the rest. He told me they would be very much offended *if I made such a fool of myself as to wade through this Valley."*

"What a pompous ass. Did you tell him where to go?"

"I told him that those folk were no friends of mine. They are actually my cousins, or second cousins or something, but they disowned me when I announced I was going on this pilgrimage. Apparently, I'm an embarrassment to the family. Anyway, I told DISCONTENT he was wrong about the valley: *for before Honour is Humility and a haughty Spirit before a fall.* So I informed him he was short in the wisdom area."

"Did you meet anybody else?"

"After that, I met this chap called SHAME," said FAITHFUL. "Very clever, a university lecturer in economics, apparently. *But of all the men that I met with in my pilgrimage, he, I think, bears the wrong name.* He was completely shameless."

# 17 SHAMELESS

FAITHFUL took a large bite of cake. "At least DISCONTENT would listen to an argument and change his mind, but SHAME could never bring himself to admit he was wrong."

"What did he say to you? Tell me when you've finished your mouthful."

A child at the table next to them calmly threw his orange juice over his mother, and CHRISTIAN watched with amusement an object lesson in bad parenting.

After a gulp of Earl Grey, FAITHFUL continued: "He objected to religion itself. *He said it was a pitiful, low, sneaking business for a man to mind Religion.* He said to be concerned about morality was a sign of weakness. An alpha male doesn't let himself be held back by a conscience. Accepting any constraints on your freedom of behaviour makes you look a fool in this age of enlightened self-interest, he said. He pointed out that very few of the mighty, rich or wise were religious.

"According to SHAME, it's quite irrational to give up the things of the world for an uncertain future. He also pointed out that pilgrims were generally of *base and low estate and condition*, and were deficient in their understanding of science and anthropology and were unlikely ever to be elected members of the Royal Society."

"Oh," said CHRISTIAN.

"He said *it was a shame to sit whining and mourning under a Sermon, and a shame to come sighing and groaning home. That it was a shame to ask my neighbour forgiveness for petty faults, or to make restitution where I have taken from any*. He believed religion made a man fail to curry favour with the great and good, merely because they have a few vices (he had some nicer names for these particular qualities).

"Instead, the religious man spends too much time mixing with the common types, just because they share his faith. And that, he said, is a shame."

"And what did you say to him?" asked CHRISTIAN.

"He made me so mad, I could not think of anything to say at first," said FAITHFUL. "But then I thought of the words in Luke 16:15: **'For that which is highly esteemed among men is abomination in the sight of God.'** *And I thought again, this SHAME tells me what men are, but it tells me nothing what God or the Word of God is.*

"On the Day of Judgment, it will be the wisdom of God that is the standard, not the wisdom of the world. So *what God says is best indeed, is best,* even if all the lecturers in all the universities in all the world are against it.

"So I said to SHAME: 'Since God prefers his religion; since God prefers a tender conscience; since those who make themselves fools for the Kingdom of Heaven are wisest; and since the poor man who loves Christ is richer than the greatest man in the world that hates him – *SHAME, depart! thou art an enemy to my salvation!*

" 'How can I listen to you rather than my King? How can I look him in the face at his coming if I am now ashamed of his ways and his servants? How could I expect any blessing?'

"But SHAME was a pain – I could not get rid of him. He kept on and on about the inadequacy of people who need the crutch of religion, and in the end I told him he was wasting his time. As far as I was concerned, all the things he despised were the things that for me had the most value. At last he tired of me, and went on his own way.

"He really wound me up, and to calm down I walked along singing a song I learned at New Wine last year:

*'The Trials that those men do meet withal,*
*That are obedient to the heavenly call,*
*Are manifold and suited to the flesh.*
*And come, and come, and come again afresh;*
*That now or sometime else, we by them may*
*Be taken, overcome, and cast away.*
*O let the Pilgrims, let the Pilgrims then,*
*Be vigilant, and quit themselves like Men.'"*

"Well done!" said CHRISTIAN. "I agree with you that he has the wrong name. He tries to put us to shame, and to make us ashamed of what is good, but he can only do this so aggressively if he himself has no shame. But never mind, however bullishly he says it, we know he is trying to glorify the foolish. Remember Proverbs 3:35: **'The wise shall inherit glory, but shame shall be the promotion of fools'**."

The Pilgrims could see that the child at the next table had been looking thoughtfully in their direction, and now had a rather large Knickerbocker Glory as a potential missile. They pushed their chairs back and left quickly.

*"I think that we must cry to him for help against SHAME,"* said FAITHFUL, *"that would have us to be valiant for Truth upon the earth."*

"Quite right," responded CHRISTIAN. "And did you meet anybody else in that valley? No hideous scaly monsters?"

*"No, not I, for I had Sun-shine all the rest of the way, through that, and also through the Valley of the Shadow of Death."*

“You were luckier than me,” said CHRISTIAN. “I had a desperate fight with APOLLYON, *but I cried to God, and he heard me, and delivered me out of all my troubles.* Then I, too, went into the Valley of the Shadow of Death, but there was no light for almost half the way through it. I thought it would be the end of me, but at last the dawn arrived, and the sun rose and the way became a lot easier.”

I could see in my dream that they were now on a wide path that was leading down to a canal. They could see a couple of longboats moored by the towpath, and in the distance there was a busy lock and a stone aqueduct.

Walking parallel with them, about fifty metres away, was a nattily-dressed man, named TALKATIVE. He was tall, and looked impressive from a distance, though less so close up.

FAITHFUL shouted over to him: “Hey, my friend, are you going to the heavenly country as we are?”

"Ooh, yes I am,” said TALKATIVE.

# 18 TALKATIVE

"Why don't you join us?" said FAITHFUL. "We can talk about the deep mysteries of our King as we walk along the towpath."

"How thrilling," said TALKATIVE, coming over to them. "I do love to talk with anybody about things that are really worthwhile." He clapped his hands together, and went on, "Actually, I have to say that I don't often come across people who want to spend time in real conversation. It does worry me that people are so trivial."

"How right you are," said FAITHFUL, eagerly, "for what better thing is there to talk about than the ways of God?"

"My dear man," said TALKATIVE, who was certainly chatty, "I do like you, you speak with such conviction, and I would simply ask what is more pleasant or profitable than theology? What could be more delightful? If a person has an interest in *the History, or the Mystery of things,* or in *Miracles, Wonders, or Signs,* then where would *he find things recorded so delightful, and so sweetly penned as in the Holy Scriptures?"*

"That's true," said FAITHFUL. "But the point is to learn something from what we talk about."

"Exactly," said TALKATIVE, "having a little chat about such matters is ever so profitable, for this is how we all learn about so much: the vanity of the world below, and the blessings of things above, and especially *the necessity of the New Birth, the insufficiency of our works, the need of Christ's righteousness,* and so forth. We also learn what it means to repent, to believe, to pray or to suffer. We learn how to find comfort in *the great Promises and Consolations of the Gospel;* and we learn how to *refuse false Opinions, vindicate the truth and instruct the ignorant."*

"I couldn't agree more," said FAITHFUL, enthusiastically.

"Isn't it tragic that so few people understand the need of faith, and the necessity of a work of grace in their soul, in order to gain eternal life?" asked TALKATIVE. "So many people are ignorantly living solely by the law, which is not the way to enter the Kingdom of Heaven."

"Yes, but *heavenly knowledge of these is the gift of God,"* said FAITHFUL. "We can't attain it by our own efforts or just by talking about it."

"I know, I know, how right you are," said TALKATIVE, *"for a man can receive nothing except it be given him from Heaven – all is of Grace, not of works.* I could quote you a hundred scriptures to confirm the truth of this."

"So what shall we talk about now?" asked FAITHFUL.

"Whatever you like," said TALKATIVE, with a sweep of his arm in the direction of the horizon. *"I will talk of things heavenly, or things earthly; things Moral, or things Evangelical; things sacred, or things profane; things past, or things to come; things foreign, or things at home; things more essential, or things circumstantial.*

"But first I need a pee, and I am going to have a little tinkle behind the trees over there before we get to the lock."

As TALKATIVE tripped away towards the trees, CHRISTIAN and FAITHFUL continued walking towards the lock where they intended to wait for TALKATIVE to catch up.

FAITHFUL said to CHRISTIAN, *"What a brave companion have we got! Surely this man will make a very excellent Pilgrim."*

CHRISTIAN smiled ruefully, and said, "I am not so sure."

"Do you know him?"

"Unfortunately I do," replied CHRISTIAN. "His name is TALKATIVE, and he lives in our town: I would have thought you would have met him, but I suppose it is a large town. He is the son of SAY-WELL; he used to live in Prating-Row, and in spite of his gift of the gab, he hasn't done much with his life."

"Oh," said FAITHFUL, surprised. "He's very presentable and well turned out."

"Only to those who don't know him," said CHRISTIAN. "He may seem presentable, but he's more like an impressionist painter whose work looks good from a distance, but close up is a mess of coloured blobs."

"Come on, you're joking, I saw you smile," said FAITHFUL.

"I'm not joking and I'm not making baseless accusations," protested CHRISTIAN. "TALKATIVE's problem is that he can talk about anything to anybody in any place. He will hold forth about theology to you, he'll talk about sport in the pub, and the more he drinks the more he talks. *Religion hath no place in his heart, or house, or conversation; all he hath lieth in his tongue, and his Religion is to make a noise therewith."*

"Well, he deceived me," said FAITHFUL.

"Deceived?" said CHRISTIAN, "you certainly are. *Remember the proverb, 'They say, and do not; but* **the Kingdom of God is not in word, but in power***'.* That's in my Book in I Corinthians 4:20.

"TALKATIVE talks the talk of prayer, repentance, faith, and new birth; but he does not walk the walk.

“I used to play football with one of his sons, and have seen him at home and at work. *His house is as empty of Religion as the white of an egg is of savour*. His dog serves God better than he does. He doesn’t pray, and he has no compunction in doing exactly what suits his selfish purpose.

“You should hear what his neighbours say about him: *‘A saint abroad, and a devil at home’,* and that is exactly what his poor family and his employees have to put up with. He’s rude and capricious; constantly berating them for something they have or haven’t done.

“He calls himself a businessman, but people who have tried to do deals with him say they would prefer to do business with the Russian Mafia. TALKATIVE is about as trustworthy as Gollum, and he teaches his children to be the same. If they show any signs of having a conscience, he calls them stupid blockheads and mocks them in front of other people.”

CHRISTIAN paused, before concluding angrily: “I think that *he has by his wicked life caused many to stumble and fall, and will be, if God prevents not, the ruin of many more.”*

“I have to believe you,” said FAITHFUL, “not just because you know him, but because, *like a Christian, you make your reports of men*. I am sure you are not saying this maliciously, but because it is true.”

“If I had not known him,” continued CHRISTIAN, “and heard about him only from *enemies to Religion* I would have assumed it was slander. But I know many bad things about him, and other people whose opinions I value have nothing good to say about him.”

“Well,” said FAITHFUL, “I must remember that saying and doing are two different things.”

“Absolutely,” said CHRISTIAN. “Just as the body without the soul is only a dead carcass, words on their own are a dead carcass too. The soul of religion is the practical part. As it says in my Book in James 1:27: **'Pure religion, undefiled before God and the Father, is this: to visit the fatherless and widows in their affliction, and to keep himself unspotted from the world'**."

They had reached the lock, where a large crowd of walkers had stopped to watch the water level go down, taking a rather flashy longboat with it.

There was a sudden scream when the parents on the side of the lock realised that they were both up above and their two young children were alone in the boat, which was now sinking into the depths of the lock. Each had thought the other was on board.

Pandemonium ensued, but there were plenty of people to help, so CHRISTIAN and FAITHFUL carried on with their discussion while they waited for TALKATIVE.

"TALKATIVE thinks hearing and saying will make him a good Christian, but he is kidding himself. Hearing is simply the sowing of the seed; talking is not enough proof that the seed has grown and borne fruit and, let's face it, *at the day of Doom men shall be judged according to their fruit.*

"At the final reckoning, the issue will not be, 'Did you believe?' but, *'Were you Doers, or Talkers only?'.* At harvest time, only the fruit matters. All TALKATIVE's fine words will be irrelevant on that day."

FAITHFUL pondered. "This reminds me of that bit in Leviticus where Moses describes the beast that is clean," he said. "Do you remember? The clean ones have both split hoofs and chew the cud. The hare chews the cud, but is unclean because it does not have a split hoof. TALKATIVE is like that*: he cheweth the Cud, he seeketh knowledge, he cheweth upon the Word; but he divideth not the hoof, he parteth not with the way of sinners."*

"I am sure that is *the true Gospel sense of those Texts,*" said

CHRISTIAN, "and I would add something else. Paul describes some people as *'sounding brass and tinkling cymbals' or 'things without life, giving sound',* as he puts it. These are people without the true faith and grace of the Gospel, who will never have a place in the kingdom of heaven, even though they can talk like an angel."

"Oh no," groaned FAITHFUL, "here he comes. I quite enjoyed talking to him at first, but now he makes me feel ill. How can we get rid of him?"

"I have a suggestion," said CHRISTIAN. "Perhaps you can make him sick of your company and he will leave us alone, unless God touches his heart through you and he changes his ways."

"What do you suggest?" asked FAITHFUL.

"Start a conversation with him about the power of religion," said CHRISTIAN. "If he goes along with you, which I am sure he will, then ask him straight whether faith is really in his heart and his house, or just in his conversation."

TALKATIVE had stopped to watch the action, and was quickly in conversation with people in the crowd. As the drama ended and the longboat emerged from the lock, he said his farewells and set off along the path to join the Pilgrims.

# 19 WHAT'S SO OBVIOUS ABOUT GRACE?

"Coo-eee! What a relief!" TALKATIVE waved a purple handkerchief at the Pilgrims, who were waiting for him along the path. "Now we can get on with some <u>serious</u> talking, my friends."

"All done, then?" asked FAITHFUL, taking him by the arm and pulling him ahead. "You asked me to choose a topic, so here it is: *How doth the saving Grace of God discover itself, when it is in the heart of men?*"

"Oh goody-goody," said TALKATIVE, "you want to talk *about the power of things*; what a really <u>super</u> question, and here's my answer in brief. First, when the grace of God is in your heart, it raises a great protest against sin. Secondly…"

"Wait a minute," said FAITHFUL, "one thing at a time. Surely God's grace shows itself by prompting the soul to hate its sins."

"But what's the difference between protesting against sin and hating sin?"

"A world of difference," said FAITHFUL. "You can easily condemn sin, but you cannot be disgusted by it unless the Spirit of God moves you.

"I have heard plenty of televangelists and preachers who condemn the sins of others, but seem to be able to tolerate their own sins in their heart, their home and even their conversation.

"Remember Potiphar's wife: she shrieked to protect her virtue but would happily have bedded Joseph. Some treat sin like a mother who calls her child a naughty girl, and then gives her a big hug."

"You're trying to catch me out," said TALKATIVE.

"Not at all," said FAITHFUL, "I simply want to get things straight. But what's your second sign that grace is at work in the heart?"

"*Great knowledge of Gospel-Mysteries,"* intoned TALKATIVE.

"You should have listed that one first," said FAITHFUL, "but first or last it is wrong. You can know every chapter and verse in the Bible but still have *no work of grace in the soul* and not be a child of God.

"When Jesus said: *'Do you know all these things?'* and the disciples answered: 'Yes', he added, *'Blessed are ye if ye do them!'* The blessing is in the doing, not the knowing.

"So, I think you are wrong. Knowledge doesn't make you a Christian. 'Knowing' is for *Talkers and Boasters,* but 'Doing' is what pleases God.

"Of course, the heart has to be informed. There's knowledge and knowledge – one is having the facts, but the other is *knowledge that is accompanied with the grace of faith and love*. This is what motivates the heart to do the will of God: the other is for the debating society. This is the knowledge that brings true contentment, the understanding that leads to obedience of God's law."

TALKATIVE was getting annoyed. "You're trying to catch me out again," he sniffed. "You're not really interested in an edifying debate."

"Alright," said FAITHFUL, "give me another example of how we find grace at work."

"No," TALKATIVE said, crossly, "because I can see we are not going to agree."

"Shall I propose one?" asked FAITHFUL.

"Feel free," TALKATIVE huffed, looking around to see how he could escape. A hot-air balloon was coming up the valley towards them, advertising a fireplace manufacturer called 'Amazing Grates'.

"A work of grace in the soul can be observed, both by the individual and other people," said FAITHFUL, getting into his stride.

"The person who has it knows he has it because he comes to realise that he is sinful. He recognises the bad things he has done in life and his lack of belief. He knows *he is sure to be damned* without the mercy of God through faith in Jesus Christ. This realisation makes him ashamed of his sin.

"But he finds within himself *the Saviour of the world, and the absolute necessity of closing with him for life*; he longs to know him more, and to experience the outcome of the promises Christ makes to him. He finds that his joy and peace are proportional to his faith in Jesus, his longing for holiness, his desire to know Christ more, and his desire to serve him in this world."

FAITHFUL paused for a minute in his flow of enthusiasm. "But it is not always easy for someone to see this as a work of grace. Sometimes the fallen nature misinterprets feelings of guilt, and you need sound judgment and a steady mind to see this for the work of grace that it is."

They walked in silence for a bit, and then FAITHFUL carried on: "Other people can also see this work of grace in the soul in two ways:

"For a start, they see the person make a *confession of his faith in Christ.* Secondly, they see the person living his life in accordance with that faith, in other words, living a life of holiness:

***heart-holiness,***
***family-holiness*** *(if he hath a family), and by*
***conversation-holiness*** *in the world.*

"**Heart holiness** means that he is inwardly rejecting his sins.

"**Family holiness** is all about bringing up his own family to live by the same standards.

"**Conversation holiness** means to *promote holiness in the world* – not simply by talking about it in a superficial, hypocritical way, but by acting, with faith and love, to put the Word of God into practice."

FAITHFUL stood to one side to let two young riders overtake them. Their horses looked bored, but perked up a bit when they sensed that TALKATIVE did not like animals.

"That's my brief description of the work of grace. What do you think? Do you disagree? If not, can I put a second question?"

"No no, far be it from me to object," said TALKATIVE, grumpily. "Just give me your second question."

"Right," said FAITHFUL, "this is what I want to know: has God done a work of grace in <u>your</u> soul? Does your life demonstrate the reality of this?

"Or is *your religion in word or tongue, and not in Deed and Truth?* Give me a simple answer that *God above will say 'Amen' to*; an answer with a clear conscience. Remember it's wrong to claim something for yourself that your neighbours know is a lie*."*

TALKATIVE went red, and did not seem to know what to say. He blew his nose, and recovered his poise.

"I have to say I did not expect to have this sort of conversation, and I don't see why I should reply," he said. "Who made you my interrogator and judge? You talk of experience and conscience, and appeal to God for verification. Why are you asking me such questions?"

"Because you were so keen to talk but I suspected you had nothing more to offer than words," said FAITHFUL, sadly. "I had heard you were someone whose religion is all mouth and no trousers. You call yourself a Christian, but you are bringing religion into disrepute. Some people have already been put off Christianity by your inconsistencies, and many more are in danger of having their faith destroyed.

"They look at you, who claims publicly to be a good Christian, and they see your boozing, your greed, your dirty jokes, your swearing, your lying and your vanity.

"You drag religion down with you! Just as people say of a prostitute that *'she is a shame to all women',* so you are a shame to all followers of Christ."

"You should take no notice of rumours," said TALKATIVE, indignantly, "and you should not rush to judgment. I don't know what your problem is, but you obviously have issues and I'm not going to waste my time talking to you. Goodbye!"

He flounced off down a sidetrack, failing to avoid some horse manure, and FAITHFUL stood watching him as he headed off into the sunset.

CHRISTIAN came up to join FAITHFUL and said: "I told you so. He couldn't reconcile your words with his selfishness. He preferred to walk away rather than reform his life.

"But he is gone – let him go, it is his loss, not ours, and he has saved us the trouble of finding an excuse to part company. He would have been a blot on our landscape and we're better off without him. As the Apostle says, *'From such withdraw thyself.'"*

FAITHFUL was still concerned about what had happened.

"I am trying to be glad we spent time with him," he said. "Perhaps he will think again about what I said. I tried to be as clear as I possibly could, so I do not think I can be held responsible if he perishes out here."

"You were right to speak plainly," CHRISTIAN said, firmly. "I wish more people would speak out nowadays, but there seems to be a fear that stating the truth might offend people. This cowardice actually *makes Religion to stink so in the Nostrils of many.* All those people in our fellowships who talk the talk but clearly do not walk the walk are undermining Christian faith and making the honest believers unhappy.

"I wish everyone would speak out like you did, so that either the hypocrites change their ways and become genuine Talker-Walkers or they find *the company of Saints would be too hot for them.* So come along, onward and upward."

FAITHFUL said: "What was that song we learned at Keswick, the one with the Welsh sounding tune? I have some new words to add:

*'How TALKATIVE at first lifts up his Plumes!*
*How bravely doth he speak! How he presumes*
*To drive down all before him! But so soon*
*As FAITHFUL talks of Heart-work like the Moon,*
*That's past the full, into the Wane he goes:*
*And so will all, but he that Heart-work knows.'"*

*Thus they went on, talking of what they had seen by the way; and so made that way easy, which would otherwise no doubt have been tedious to them: for now they went through a Wilderness.*

## TIME FOR A COFFEE BREAK

If we are on the right road, does it matter how we got onto it?

How can you spot a Christian? Clothes? Mark? Roll?

Once a Christian, always a Christian? What do you think Bunyan meant by the incident of CHRISTIAN losing his Roll?

There were quite a number of relics from the Book of Judges in the Palace Beautiful. How do you understand the genocide and brutalities in the Bible?

How did Jesus and Paul understand the nature of the devil, the destroyer, the accuser? How should we understand this today?

Have you ever sat *whining and mourning under a Sermon*? How should the church teach the faith?

***'Judge not, that ye be not judged'*** (Matthew 7:1)
CHRISTIAN makes quite a lot of condemning judgments about Talkative. What is the difference between the discernment that is part of wisdom and the judgment that is condemned by Jesus?

What is integrity, and how do you ensure that you walk what you talk? Is integrity relative to the environment? Can one person have conflicting integrities which are each true in each place where they are exercised?

'Family Holiness' – Samuel and David were not great parents, judged by their children. Is that a fair criticism?

You know how to maintain your physical and mental wellbeing, but how do you improve and maintain your spiritual wellbeing?

How would you explain the idea of 'grace' to a modern teenager?

# 20 ONE OF YOU IS GOING TO DIE

At last the landscape began to change, and they could see that they were leaving the Wilderness. Looking back, FAITHFUL spotted somebody coming after them. “Who’s that?” he wondered.

CHRISTIAN shaded his eyes to see and exclaimed, “It’s my good friend, EVANGELIST.”

“He’s my good friend, too,” said FAITHFUL. “He is the one who set me on the path to the Gate.”

They waited as EVANGELIST caught up, and they greeted each other warmly. “So what has been happening to you both on your journey so far?” asked EVANGELIST.

CHRISTIAN and FAITHFUL told him how grateful they were for all his guidance, and they described the encounters and the difficulties they had met along the way.

“I am glad,” said EVANGELIST, “not that you had so many trials, but that you overcame them and did not give up, despite your mistakes. I am glad for my sake, too. *I have sowed, and you have reaped; and the day is coming when both he that sowed and they that reaped shall rejoice together.*

“But,” he added, “you must keep going. You will gain your reward, as long as you don’t lose heart. *The crown is before you;*

*and it is an incorruptible one.* Run after it and don't let anyone snatch it from you."

They came to a bridge across a stream, and sitting down for a drink and a rest, EVANGELIST continued with a warning. *"You are not yet out of the Gun-shot of the Devil; you have not resisted unto blood, striving against sin. Let the Kingdom be always before you; and believe steadfastly concerning things that are invisible."*

They could see a pike in the water below, immobile, watching and waiting. They sat staring into the water, curious to see what it would do.

After a while, EVANGELIST continued: "Do not let yourselves fall prey to worldly values. Above all, look into your own hearts and be aware of your own desires, for they are the most deceitful of all and desperately wicked. *Set your faces like a flint; you have all power in heaven and earth on your side."*

EVANGELIST offered them some chocolate, and while they were dividing it up, CHRISTIAN caught FAITHFUL's eye. The Pilgrims knew that EVANGELIST *was a Prophet and could tell them of things that might happen unto them; and also how they might resist and overcome them.* They also both sensed some concern in his words.

CHRISTIAN asked hesitantly: "So can you tell what might happen to us both? How can we overcome these trials that I think you see ahead of us?"

EVANGELIST looked thoughtful. "*My sons*, you know that it is through many tribulations that we enter the Kingdom of Heaven," he said. "You also know the pitfalls that commerce and politics bring – the obligations and pressures, the deals and deceit. Everyone who starts on this journey finds this out sooner rather than later.

"You know something of this already, but you are now approaching a town where Pilgrims have many enemies, who will go all out to kill you.

"I know that one of you will die there...

*...but be you faithful unto death, and the King will give you a Crown of Life.*

"The one who dies, although his death will be unjust and his pain perhaps great, he will be the more fortunate one of you two. Not only will he arrive first at the Celestial City, but he will also escape the many miseries that the other one will encounter on the rest of his journey.

"However, when you reach this town and you find my prophecy is true, remember me and remember Bishop Latimer and Master Ridley: play the man, *quit yourselves like men*, entrust your souls to God, your *faithful Creator.*"

# 21 VANITY FAIR

*Then I saw in my dream*, that as they walked along the road they passed a sign that announced, 'Welcome to Vanity – Shop 'til you Drop'.

They began to enter the suburbs of a large town and all around them the traffic increased. As they came over the brow of a hill they could see below them the glass-fronted blocks of the commercial centre glinting in the sunlight. EVANGELIST had told them that this shopping mall by the Castle Mound was the largest in the region, and had been nick-named 'Vanity Fair'.

The shopping mall stood on a site that had been a market-place for centuries. Three early City Fathers, BEELZEBUB, APOLLYON and LEGION, noticing that the town was on the Pilgrim path, started the first market, which quickly turned into a year-long event. You could buy anything there: *houses, lands, trades, places, honours, preferments, titles, countries, kingdoms; lusts, pleasures, and delights of all sorts, whores, bawds, wives, husbands, children, masters, servants, lives, blood, bodies, souls, silver, gold, pearls, precious stones, and what not.*

The Fair attracted all sorts of *Jugglings, Cheats, Games, Plays, Fools, Apes, Knaves, and Rogues.* It was a rats' nest of theft, murder, adultery and lies.

To add to the attractions, it was an international market, where traders congregated by nationality. There was a British row, a French row, an Italian row, a Spanish row and a German row, all offering their authentic national vanities. *As in other Fairs, some one Commodity is as the chief of all the Fair, so the ware of Rome and her merchandise is greatly promoted in this Fair: only our English nation, with some others, have taken a dislike thereat.*

There was no avoiding Vanity Fair, because the road to the Celestial City went straight through it.

The *Prince of Princes* himself passed this way, when he came through the town en route to his own country. BEELZEBUB, Chief Lord of the Fair, invited him to stop and browse. He promised to make him Lord of the Fair, if he would only show BEELZEBUB reverence in front of the stallholders. BEELZEBUB was so pleased to have such an illustrious visitor that he took him from street to street, hoping the *Blessed One* would give in to temptation and buy one of his vanities. But he had no interest in the merchandise and he left the town without laying out so much as a single penny.

So clearly the Fair is a very ancient event, of long standing, and an impressive commercial enterprise.

As CHRISTIAN and FAITHFUL entered the shopping mall, they became conscious that people were staring at them. They realised that their clothes were very different from everyone else's.

"Hmm, wearing Grandpa's cast offs," they heard someone mutter.

But, in fact, they could understand very little of what people were saying. Most of the crowd seemed to speak a different language – indeed several different languages, so that there was a babble of voices, unable to comprehend one another.

But what caused most amusement was the fact that the Pilgrims had no interest in buying anything. When any salesman tried to talk them into a deal, CHRISTIAN and FAITHFUL would *put their fingers in their ears, and cry, "Turn away mine eyes from beholding Vanity," and look upwards, signifying that their trade and traffic was in heaven.*

Someone shouted out as they passed, "You have to buy something!"

CHRISTIAN responded: *"We buy the truth".*

There were shouts of laughter and abuse, and somebody yelled out, "Kick him in the head, the pillock!"

At this point the crowd began to turn nasty, and several security guards came running. CHRISTIAN and FAITHFUL were bundled into a van and driven to the shopping mall Management Office.

Here, the Centre Manager regarded them with suspicion. "What are you doing here? Why aren't you buying anything?" he insisted. "Why are you dressed so oddly? Are you Irish travellers? Are you asylum seekers?"

CHRISTIAN and FAITHFUL protested that they were simply Pilgrims from out of town, *and that they were going to their own Country, which was the heavenly Jerusalem.* They had done nothing to cause offence to anyone, and had merely said they were only interested in buying the truth.

The Centre Manager did not believe them, and called in a couple of journalists and a TV camera crew to interview them.

The regional news rushed out a breathless documentary – **"Madmen or Saboteurs? We Expose the Truth about the Suspicious Strangers in our Midst!"** Some said they were dangerous lunatics; others claimed they were industrial spies, sent by rival commercial barons to undermine the economy of Vanity. They became fair game for any sort of abuse or ridicule on chat shows or in stand-up comedy routines.

But CHRISTIAN and FAITHFUL refused to retaliate, and tried to find ways to turn the abuse around so that they could somehow bless their tormentors. They sought to find ways of doing acts of kindness for those who laughed at them.

Some of the more thoughtful, less prejudiced people in Vanity began to notice this, and letters started appearing in the press criticising those who were driving the attacks.

The correspondents pointed out that the two men were peaceful and, as far as they could see, intended no harm to anybody. "I can think of people in this town who are more deserving of a spell in jail," remarked one correspondent, darkly. This led to a furious exchange on the letters pages and several fights in pubs.

The Manager of the Shopping Mall decided that CHRISTIAN and FAITHFUL were entirely to blame for the fracas, even though they themselves had urged only peace and calm. The Manager talked to the Chief Constable, who then sent a file to the Crown Prosecution Service. It was decided the situation had to be dealt with, to demonstrate that the authorities in the town had a firm grip on law and order. CHRISTIAN and FAITHFUL were arrested and put in the police cells.

But there they behaved with such patience and dignity that many more people were moved to support them. The authorities were furious. They vowed the two men *should die for the abuse they had done, and for deluding the men of the Fair.*

As they sat together in their cell, the two men remembered what EVANGELIST had said, and took encouragement from this. They reminded each other that the one who would suffer would have the better deal, and each secretly hoped it would be him that would be taken first. But they entrusted their fate to God and waited calmly for what should unfold.

A date for the trial was set, and CHRISTIAN and FAITHFUL were taken to court to appear before Mr Justice HATEGOOD. They were charged with disturbance of the peace, conspiracy to disrupt lawful trade and the spreading of seditious opinions, contrary to the law of the King.

# 22 THE TRIAL

FAITHFUL was asked first whether he pleaded guilty or not guilty. He replied that all he had done was oppose the power that opposes God.

"As for disturbing the peace," he said, "I did no such thing, being myself a man of peace. The only reason some people came to support our cause is that they could see we were innocent and spoke the truth. *And as to the King you talk of, since he is BEELZEBUB, the enemy of our Lord, I defy him and all his Angels."*

The judge asked if there were any witnesses to be called for the prosecution, and was told there were three. First to be called was ENVY, who stood up and said*: "My lord, I have known this man a long time; and will attest upon my oath before this Honourable Bench, that he is..."*

The judge interrupted, "Wait! He hasn't taken the oath."

Once he was sworn in, ENVY continued, "My lord, despite his pleasant sounding name, this FAITHFUL is one of the worst men you can find. He has no respect for authority, nor for ordinary, decent people; he takes no notice of law or custom. He does everything he can to spread his seditious notions, which he has the nerve to call '*Principles of Faith and Holiness'.*

"I actually heard him say once that Christianity and the ways of our Town of Vanity were diametrically opposed and could not be reconciled. In other words, my Lord, he treats with contempt not only all our worthy enterprises but us, too, for doing them."

"Is that it?" asked the judge.

"My lord, I could say much more but I don't want to take up the court's valuable time. Hear the other witnesses, and if you need more, I have plenty to give."

The second witness to be called was a mysterious lady called Ms SUPERSTITION. She had long hair and clanked as she walked, from the number of crystal pendants strung around her neck. She was asked to look at the prisoner, take the oath, and give her evidence against him.

"My lord," said Ms SUPERSTITION, "I do not really know this man, nor do I want to. He has a troubled aura which gives me a headache. However, I did have a recent conversation with him and I found he had a very negative vibe. He said our religion was rubbish, and could not please God; he thinks we are sinners and heading for damnation. What more do I need to say?"

A witness named PICKTHANK was then called. He hurried eagerly to the witness box, delighted to have this opportunity to curry favour with the authorities. "I've known the prisoner a long time, and I've heard him say some disgraceful things," he said in shocked tones. "He's lambasted our noble Prince BEELZEBUB and criticised his honourable friends, *the Lord OLDMAN, the Lord CARNAL DELIGHT, the Lord LUXURIOUS, the Lord DESIRE OF VAIN GLORY, my old Lord LECHERY, Sir HAVING GREEDY* and all the rest of our esteemed nobility.

"What is worse," went on PICKTHANK, "he called you, my Lord, '*an ungodly Villain*', and his mud-slinging has bespattered the good name of the leaders in our community."

Looking directly at the prisoner at the bar, the judge said: "Well, you *Runagate, Heretic, and Traitor,* what do you think of what these honest people have said about you?"

FAITHFUL slowly stood up and said: “Can I say a few words in my own defence?”

“Frankly, Sir,” said the Judge, “I think you ought to be shot immediately in front of your family, but so that people can see how just and merciful we are, you can say a few words, you miserable wretch.”

Sensing that he was fighting a losing battle, FAITHFUL nevertheless spoke out firmly and boldly. “In response to Mr ENVY, all I have ever said is that any rule, law, custom or people that is directly against the Word of God, is diametrically opposite to Christianity. If I am wrong in this belief, convince me of my error and I will admit it.

“As for the accusation of Ms SUPERSTITION, what I actually said was this: to worship God you must have divine faith; but there can be no divine faith without a divine revelation of the will of God. If you bring into the worship of God things which are not part of divine revelation, but are some human invention, that faith will not lead to eternal life.

“As for what Mr PICKTHANK said, I repeat, calmly, my belief that the prince of this town and all his hangers-on *are more fit for being in hell than in this town and country; and so the Lord have mercy upon me!”*

All this time, the jury had been listening to the witnesses. Now the Judge told them they had to decide whether to condemn FAITHFUL or save his life, but first he would remind them of the law in this matter.

“In the days of Pharaoh the Great, servant to our prince,” said the Judge, “an act was passed such that if adherents of another religion should multiply and threaten the status quo, their male children should be thrown into the river.

"Nebuchadnezzar the Great, another of our great prince's servants, decreed that any person who would not fall down and worship his golden image should be thrown into a blast furnace. Another legal precedent is the decision made in the days of Darius, whereby whoever called upon any God but his should be cast into a den of lions."

The Judge turned and glowered at FAITHFUL. Taking off his glasses, he said: "These laws have been broken, not only in thought, but also in word and deed. This is intolerable. In the case of Pharaoh's law it is worth noting that his law was enforced even though there was no crime committed, only a supposition that a crime *might* be committed.

"But in the case before us a crime has clearly been committed. It definitely falls under the second and third acts I have cited, as the prisoner criticised our religion and admits it. This is treason, and he deserves to die."

The jury went out to deliberate, and the foreman, Mr BLIND-MAN, said, *"I see clearly that this man is a heretic."* They went round the table:

Mr NO-GOOD said: *"Away with such a fellow from the earth!"*

*"Aye," said Mr MALICE, "for I hate the very looks of him."*

Mr LOVE-LUST sniffed, *"I could never endure him."*

*"Nor I,"* said Mr LIVE-LOOSE, *"for he would always be condemning my way."*

*"Hang him, hang him!"* urged Mr HEADY.

*"A sorry scrub,"* said Mr HIGH-MIND.

*"My heart riseth against him,"* added Mr ENMITY.

*"He is a rogue,"* said Mr LIAR.

*"Hanging is too good for him,"* shouted Mr CRUELTY.

*"Let's dispatch him out of the way,"* said Mr HATE-LIGHT.

Finally, Mr IMPLACABLE said, *"Might I have all the world given me, I could not be reconciled to him; therefore let us bring him guilty of death."*

And so they did.

He was condemned to be taken out and put to the cruelest death that could be invented, according to their law. First they flogged him, then beat him and slit his flesh with knives. Then they stoned him, stabbed him with their swords, and finally burned him to ashes at the stake.

That is how FAITHFUL met his end.

*Now I saw that there stood behind the multitude a Chariot and a couple of horses waiting for FAITHFUL, who - so soon as his adversaries had dispatched him - was taken up into it, and straightway was carried up through the Clouds, with sound of Trumpet, the nearest way to the Celestial Gate.*

As for CHRISTIAN, the court was not ready to deal with him yet, so he was remanded back to prison and remained there for a while.

But God, who overrules all things, had other plans for this Pilgrim and ensured that CHRISTIAN was able to escape his jail, flee the town and continue on his way.

And as he went he sang quietly to himself:

*'Well, FAITHFUL, thou hast faithfully professed*
*Unto thy Lord, with whom thou shalt be blessed,*
*When faithless ones, with all their vain delight,*
*Are crying out under their Hellish plight.*
*Sing, FAITHFUL, sing! -  and let thy name survive;*
*For though they killed thee, thou art yet alive.'*

# 23 HOPEFUL JOINS THE TEAM

Now I saw in my dream that CHRISTIAN was not alone as he continued along his path. As he walked sadly away from the Town of Vanity, a young man came running up to him. He was wearing a red and white tracksuit and a baseball cap, and introduced himself as HOPEFUL.

He said he had been watching CHRISTIAN and FAITHFUL in their sufferings, and had been impressed by their words and behaviour. Now he wanted to join CHRISTIAN on his journey.

CHRISTIAN gave him a hug, and they agreed to support each other through whatever lay ahead.

*Thus one died to bear Testimony to the Truth, and another rises out of the Ashes to be a Companion with CHRISTIAN in their pilgrimage.*

HOPEFUL told CHRISTIAN that he knew many more people in Vanity Fair would follow them, in due course.

As the Pilgrims hurried away from the town, they overtook a smoothly-dressed young man who was tapping away furiously on his iPad. CHRISTIAN and HOPEFUL greeted him and asked him where he was going. He told them he was travelling to the Celestial City from the Town of Fairspeech.

"From Fairspeech!" said CHRISTIAN. "Do any good and honest folk live there?"

The man looked a bit put out, and said he certainly hoped so.

"Excuse me," said CHRISTIAN, "but what is your name?"

The man laughed, and said, "I don't know you and you don't know me, but if you are travelling the same way, I shall be glad of your company. If not, then too bad."

"This Town of Fairspeech," asked CHRISTIAN, "it is quite a wealthy place, I believe?"

"It certainly is, and I have many rich friends and family there," was the response.

"Who are your family, if you don't mind my asking?" said CHRISTIAN.

"I'm connected to just about everybody, but in particular, *my Lord TURN-ABOUT; my Lord TIME-SERVER; my Lord FAIRSPEECH* (whose ancestors gave the town its name)*; also Mr. SMOOTH-MAN; Mr. FACING-BOTH-WAYS; Mr. ANY-THING; and the Parson of our parish, Mr. TWO-TONGUES, was my mother's own brother by father's side.*

"I have worked my way up society; my great-grandfather *was but a waterman, looking one way and rowing another* - and I have made my money in newspapers by doing much the same. I'm actually the leader writer on our biggest daily broadsheet, you know. I pride myself on keeping in touch with informed opinion."

CHRISTIAN asked if he was married.

"Yes indeed," was the reply. "My wife is a wonderful woman – daughter of another wonderful woman, Lady FEIGNING. She's a pure-bred aristocrat, you know, yet she can speak to the cleaning lady just as easily as she can to a prince.

"We are truly religious, but we're not like those enthusiasts. We differ from them in two small points: firstly, we never go against the flow.

"Secondly, we feel above all that religion should be popular. *We are always most zealous when religion goes in his silver slippers – we love much to walk with him in the street if the sun shines, and the people applaud it."*

CHRISTIAN turned to HOPEFUL, and said quietly, "I think this is BY-ENDS, of Fairspeech, and if I am right, we have landed ourselves with a right crook."

HOPEFUL whispered, "Go on, ask him. He shouldn't be ashamed of his name."

So CHRISTIAN turned back, and said, "Sir, you are obviously extremely knowledgeable, but am I right in guessing that you are in fact Mr. BY-ENDS, of Fairspeech?"

The journalist coughed, and said in a rather pained way, "That is not actually my real name. It is a nickname given to me by people who dislike me, you know. I put up with it, reluctantly, as other good men have had to do."

"But surely you must have done something to merit the name?"

"Never," said BY-ENDS, emphatically, "never, never! Like the Vicar of Bray, my gift has been an ability to anticipate changes and agree with them before they happen, and therefore to be in a position to benefit when they do. I consider this a blessing, not a cause for abuse."

"I thought that's who you were," nodded CHRISTIAN, "and I'm afraid you merit the name more than you think."

# 24 GOSSIP WITH A COLUMNIST

BY-ENDS shrugged his shoulders. "Well, if that's what you think, there is nothing I can do, but my car is just over there and I can give you a lift. You will find me a good companion on the journey."

"If you come with us," said CHRISTIAN, "you will have to go against the flow, and *you must also own religion in his rags as well as when in his silver slippers; and stand by him, too, when bound in irons, as well as when he walketh the streets with applause."*

"You cannot impose your views on my faith," BY-ENDS said, self-righteously. "You have to allow me freedom of belief. But let me come along with you anyway," he added.

"Sorry," said CHRISTIAN, "not a step further, unless you will do as we do."

"I cannot desert my established principles," said BY-ENDS. "They are both *harmless and profitable*. If I cannot join you, then I will either carry on by myself, or wait for others who will be glad of my company." And he stalked off to his car.

Now I saw in my dream that CHRISTIAN and HOPEFUL walked away, but before they turned a bend in the road, they looked back and saw three young men in chinos and rugby shirts approaching BY-ENDS.

They greeted him with a great deal of hand-shaking and back-slapping. All three men – HOLD-THE-WORLD, MONEY-LOVE, and SAVE-ALL – had been at the same school as BY-ENDS. They had been taught by a certain Dr GRIPEMAN, who had founded a minor public school in Love-Gain, a market town in the northern County of Coveting. They had been in the First XV together, and had all met up again at the ten-year reunion the previous year, when in a drunken spree they burnt down a historic summer house.

The school prided itself on teaching *the art of getting, either by violence, cozenage, flattery, lying, or by putting on a guise of religion.* These four old Gripemanians had learned their lessons so well that each of them could have lectured on the subject at degree level.

MONEY-LOVE, who was carrying a hockey stick, asked BY-ENDS, "Who were those two you were talking to?"

"They come from miles away, and are going on a pilgrimage," said BY-ENDS.

"What a shame they did not wait for us," said MONEY-LOVE. "Surely we are all on a pilgrimage, aren't we?"

"Absolutely," said BY-ENDS, "but those guys are so dogmatic, and totally convinced that they are the only ones who are right. They have no time for the opinions of others, however godly, and refuse to join with anybody who does not agree with them in everything."

"That's bad," said SAVE-ALL. "But one does come across people who are so sure of their own righteousness that they can only conclude everyone else must be damned! But where did they disagree with you?"

"In their blinkered way they believe it is their duty to journey in all weathers, and to go against the flow, while I believe we should wait for a favourable wind and tide."

BY-ENDS brushed some dirt off his shiny car. "They are quite prepared to risk everything they have for God, whereas I believe in the importance of safeguarding my life and my hard-earned possessions.

"They want to stand by their opinions, even if everybody else is against them. I am all for religion if the circumstances are right and my safety is not compromised. *They are for religion when in rags and contempt; but I am for him when he walks in his golden slippers in the sunshine, and with applause."*

"How right you are, BY-ENDS," said HOLD-THE-WORLD. "He is a fool who gives up what he cannot lose to gain what he cannot keep. *Let us be wise as serpents;* let's make hay when the sun shines, like the bee who sleeps in the hive all winter, and only comes out when *she can have profit with pleasure.*

"Sometimes God sends rain, and sometimes sunshine; if they want to go through the rain, we will wait for the sun.

"As for me, I prefer religion that comes with the security of God's good blessings," he said, and the others murmured their assent.

"Surely any thinking person would agree that if God has given us the good things of life, he wants us to keep them for <u>His</u> sake?"

HOLD-THE-WORLD went on: "*Abraham and Solomon grew rich in religion.* And so did Job, who said *'a good man shall lay up gold as dust',* but it doesn't sound as if those two chaps up there have much gold in the bank."

"Absolutely," said SAVE-ALL, "I think that we are all agreed, so that's that."

"Exactly, there is nothing more to say," said MONEY-LOVE. "Anyone who does not accept the authority of Scripture or reason (and we have both on our side) either doesn't know his own freedom or doesn't know how to look after his own interests."

A couple of Sloane Rangers in a Morgan roared by, waving furiously at the lads, and pointing at a pub in the distance. They all waved back and cheered.

"So, my friends," said BY-ENDS, "as we are all going on our pilgrimage together, to distract our minds away from any worries we might have, let me pose this question:

> **Suppose someone – a vicar, or a student – should see an opportunity to get the good things of life, but can only do this by being a lot more religious than he would normally be: can the means justify the end and the person still retain their integrity?"**

# 25 THE BISHOP AND THE ACTRESS

They stood thinking for a minute, and then MONEY-LOVE spoke up: "I see what you are getting at, so perhaps I may be allowed to suggest an answer?

"First, the vicar. Suppose he can see the possibility of becoming a Bishop, but to do this he has to spend more time in diocesan meetings, more time in theological study, and has to tone down his preaching about the work of the Holy Spirit to satisfy the congregation. I do not see a problem with this, providing *he has a call.* I think he could go further than this, and still hold his integrity. Why?

"1. His ambition for preferment is perfectly legal and if the opportunity has been set before him by *Providence*, he should go for it, *making no question, for conscience sake.*

"2. His ambition has actually made him more hard-working, and so makes him a better man. *Yea, makes him better improve his parts, which is according to the mind of God.*

"3. As far as the congregation is concerned, if he is willing to compromise on his theology so as not to upset them, this shows that he is a self-denying person, ready to put others first, and so even more fit for higher office.

"4. In summary, a clergyman who exchanges a parish for a diocese should not *be judged as covetous*; but rather be seen as someone who has increased his knowledge and productivity, has followed his calling, and has been given the opportunity to do good.

"As for the student: suppose she cannot get a job, but has the opportunity to join Riding Lights Theatre Company if she becomes religious. She could go on to become a great actress, get to Hollywood, become a film star, even marry a rich celebrity, perhaps. I do not see a problem with this. Why?

"1. Being religious is a virtue, whatever the road that brought you there.

"2. It is not illegal to find a rich husband, or to become a great actress.

"3. In any case, if you get good things by becoming religious, you get good things by becoming good yourself. So, she ends up with a rich husband, fame and fortune, and all by becoming religious, which is a good thing. Becoming religious to achieve all these good things, has to be a *good and profitable design."*

The others all applauded MONEY-LOVE, and told him they could not see how anyone could disagree with his analysis of the Bishop and the Actress.

Remembering CHRISTIAN and HOPEFUL, they wondered how they would answer the question, so they all jumped into BY-ENDS' car and chased after the Pilgrims. In the car they decided that HOLD-THE-WORLD should do the talking, so that there was no chance of rekindling the animosity between the Pilgrims and BY-ENDS.

The car overtook the Pilgrims, and stopped in front of them, and they all got out. After polite greetings all round, HOLD-THE-WORLD asked them the question.

"Oh, come on," said CHRISTIAN, "*Even a babe in religion may answer ten thousand such questions.* What does Jesus say in John 6? If it is wrong to follow Jesus for bread, how much more disgusting it is to *make him and religion a stalking-horse to get and enjoy the world*! Only ***heathens***, ***hypocrites***, ***devils***, *and* ***witches*** would do this. Let me demonstrate:

1. **Heathens:** In Genesis 34 is the story of Hamor and Shechem, who wanted Jacob's daughter and cattle, and saw there was no other way to get them but by being circumcised. So they persuaded all the males in their community, and they used religion as a stalking-horse to get wealth. But what happened? *Read the whole story.*

2. **Hypocrites:** The Pharisees would have agreed with you. They indulged in long prayers, but what they really wanted was to get their hands on widows' houses. Their reward was damnation from God.

3. **Devils:** *Judas the devil* tried this; he followed Jesus so he could get his fingers on the collection bag, but in the end he lost everything.

4. **Witches:** *Simon the witch* in Acts 8 would also have agreed with you. He wanted the gift of the Holy Spirit because he thought it would be a source of wealth. And read what Peter said to him.

"I should also say that if you are the sort of person to take up religion for gain, you will also probably give it up for gain. Judas became religious for greed and he sold his Master and his faith down the river for greed. Answering the question in the way you have done *is both heathenish, hypocritical, and devilish; and your reward will be according to your works."*

CHRISTIAN looked around the group to see what response he would get.

There was complete silence.

HOPEFUL was nodding thoughtfully, but the rest were motionless and silent, looking at the ground, or in the case of MONEY-LOVE, examining the handle of his hockey stick.

CHRISTIAN beckoned to HOPEFUL and they started walking on down the road, passing the parked car.

BY-ENDS and his friends watched them go, and then climbed into the car, but kept stopping and starting, as they did not want to overtake the two Pilgrims. When they reached the pub, they parked and went into the bar to find the girls.

CHRISTIAN said to HOPEFUL thoughtfully, "If these men cannot justify their actions to us, what hope do they have before God? And if they cannot give good reasons for their actions when we challenge them, *what will they do when they shall be rebuked by the flames of a devouring fire?"*

# 26 GET RICH QUICK

The road continued for some miles through a pine forest, but as they walked down an incline and round a bend, the Pilgrims saw stretching before them *a delicate plain, called Ease*. This was pleasant walking, but it did not last for long, and at the end of the plain they could see *a little hill called Lucre*.

At the bottom of the hill was a small settlement, which had grown up when silver had been discovered under the hill. Some previous Pilgrims had turned aside to mine the deposits, but the ground conditions were poor. A number of miners had been killed, and some who survived were physically and mentally scarred by the experience.

I saw in my dream, that a little way off the road was a smart white building with a sign over the main entrance: 'Demas Consolidated Mines PLC'. As the Pilgrims approached, DEMAS himself walked out to greet them.

"Good day, gentlemen," he called. "I have a very interesting proposition for you."

CHRISTIAN stopped in the road, surprised to be accosted in the middle of nowhere by a man in a three-piece suit. He looked as if he wanted to give the impression of an old style bank manager, but his lapels were a little too wide and his tie a little too loud, making him look more like a used car salesman.

"What on earth have you got that is worth our leaving the way to see?" CHRISTIAN asked.

"Why, this is a famous silver mine, and with a small investment and a bit of hard digging you can make a lot of money."

"Hey, I'd really like to see that," said HOPEFUL.

"Not me," said CHRISTIAN; "I have heard of this place, and how many have been killed in the diggings. Anyway, wealth is *a snare to those that seek it, for it hinders them in their pilgrimage*."

CHRISTIAN asked DEMAS: "Aren't the mine workings dangerous? Hasn't this place been a menace to pilgrims on their journey?"

"It is not very dangerous, unless you are careless," replied DEMAS, but he would not look CHRISTIAN in the eye, and went slightly red as he spoke.

CHRISTIAN pulled HOPEFUL's arm and frog-marched him along, telling him to keep his feet firmly on the road.

"I bet your life old BY-ENDS will take him up on the invitation," said HOPEFUL.

"I am quite sure he will," agreed CHRISTIAN, "and I bet *a hundred to one but he dies there."*

DEMAS called after them, "But this is the chance of the lifetime. At least come back and look?"

Then CHRISTIAN got a bit annoyed, and shouted back: "DEMAS, you are *an enemy to the right ways of the Lord of this way.* I know you already have a criminal conviction for breaching health and safety laws in your activities here. Why do you want to get us into trouble? If we turn off the path here, our Lord the King would certainly hear of it, and we would be ashamed when we come to stand before him."

DEMAS hurried towards them. "No, no, you have it all wrong," he said smoothly. "I am also a Pilgrim, and if you will just wait a minute, I want to come and walk with you."

"So what is your name?" asked CHRISTIAN. "Have I not got it right?"

"Yes, my name is DEMAS; *I am the son of Abraham.*"

"Oh, really?" said CHRISTIAN. "I know who you are; *Gehazi was your great-grandfather, and Judas your father,* and you have walked in their footsteps. Your get-rich-quick scheme is *but a devilish prank.* Your father came to a bad end and you will finish the same way. When we come to the King, we will tell him what you are up to."

The Pilgrims hurried along the road away from the mine.

Behind them they heard the hoot of a car horn, and there were BY-ENDS and his companions being waved over by DEMAS.

Now, whether BY-ENDS and his rugby friends went to visit the mine workings and fell over into the pit, or whether they went down to dig, or whether they were suffocated at the bottom by the firedamp and methane that was common there, I am not sure; but I did observe that they never made it back to the path.

As they walked on their way, CHRISTIAN and HOPEFUL sang some new words to a worship song they learned at the last Spring Harvest:

*"BY-ENDS and Silver DEMAS both agree,*
*One calls, the other runs that he may be*
*A sharer in his Lucre, so these do*
*Take up in this World, and no farther go."*

On the other side of the plain, the Pilgrims came across an odd monument by the side of the road. It looked like a woman trying to morph into a Corinthian column. "Perhaps it's an early Anthony

Gormley," said HOPEFUL, as they stood staring at it, trying to work out what to make of it.

HOPEFUL spotted what looked like an inscription, but it was in an odd script. "Here, CHRISTIAN, what does this say?" he asked. "You've got a GCSE in art, haven't you?"

"Er, only in technical drawing, actually," said CHRISTIAN. They peered at it and eventually deciphered the letters.

'REMEMBER LOT'S WIFE,' it read.

They realised that this must be the pillar of salt into which Lot's wife was turned *for her looking back with a covetous heart* when she was running from Sodom for safety.

CHRISTIAN and HOPEFUL sat down by the road, and CHRISTIAN pulled a couple of cans of Coke from his haversack.

"This is a salutary reminder, brother," he said, "coming as it does after our brush with DEMAS. If we had done what you wanted to do and gone back to look at the silver mine, we might also have become like this woman, a statue for pilgrims to gawp at."

"It was stupid of me," said HOPEFUL, hugging his knees. "I'm beginning to wonder if I am just like Lot's wife. What is the difference between her sin and mine? We both wanted something – all she did was look back, but I really wanted to go and see the mine. *Let Grace be adored.* I'm ashamed."

"Let's take a photo of it, to remind us in the future," said CHRISTIAN. "This woman escaped one judgment, but was destroyed by another. She missed the destruction of Sodom, but still ended up as part of a giant condiment set."

HOPEFUL was trying to work out whether to take the photo in portrait or landscape.

"True," he said. "She is both a warning and an example – a warning that we should avoid her sin, and an example of what happens if we ignore the warning. And what about Korah, Dathan and Abiram in Numbers 26, and their two hundred and fifty followers? How was that for a judgment?"

He walked around the pillar taking shots from various angles, and then took a shot back along the road towards the mine.

"What I don't understand," he said, "is how DEMAS and his cronies can be digging away for the treasure for which this woman was turned into a pillar of salt. She was only looking, for heaven's sake, but they are actually digging. From where they are they can see this column standing here. Why don't they grasp the warning?"

"Astonishing, isn't it?" said CHRISTIAN. "They must be obsessed. They are like pick pockets thieving right under the magistrate's nose.

"Genesis 13 says the men of Sodom were *'sinners before the Lord'*, – in other words, in front of his very eyes. In spite of the fact that God in his kindness had made Sodom like the Garden of Eden of old, the men persisted in their sin. *This, therefore, provoked him the more to jealousy; and made their plagues hot as the fire of the Lord out of heaven could make it.*

"When such examples are clearly set before people, and yet they deliberately sin in God's sight, they *must be partakers of severest judgments."*

HOPEFUL put his camera back in its case.

"You are quite right," he said; "what a mercy we have not suffered this fate! It is time yet again to thank God, *to fear before him; and always to 'remember Lot's wife'.*"

# 27 BY-PATH MEADOW

The path led beside a pleasant river, which King David had called '*the River of God*', but John called '*the River of the Water of Life*'. The two Pilgrims walked along the bank, and dipped their flasks in the cool water; they felt soothed and refreshed.

On either side of the river were orchards, where countless varieties of fruit trees were growing, and they discovered that the leaves of the trees had medicinal properties. They filled themselves with fruit, and chewed on a few of the leaves, to ease the aches and pains brought on by strenuous travelling. Along the bank was a meadow, green all year round and beautiful with lilies.

Seeing that this was a safe place, the weary Pilgrims pitched camp and lay down to sleep. For several days they camped beside the river, eating fruit and drinking the refreshing water.

HOPEFUL had time to practise his old mouth-organ skills, and one evening beside the fire he composed a melody to match their mood. CHRISTIAN wrote some words to go with it:

*Behold ye how these crystal streams do glide,*
*To comfort Pilgrims, by the highway side;*
*The meadows green, besides their fragrant smell,*
*Yield dainties for them: and he that can tell*
*What pleasant fruit, yea, leaves, these trees do yield,*
*Will soon sell all, that he may buy this field.*

But this was not the end of their journey, and so the time came for them to pack up and travel on.

I saw in my dream that after a short distance the path and the river parted company. The Pilgrims were disappointed, but they dared not leave the path.

But as they went on, it became heavily rutted and rocky, their weary feet began to blister, and they got rapidly disheartened.

On the left of the path they could see a soft meadow, called 'By-Path Meadow', and when they came to a stile, CHRISTIAN said: "If this field runs parallel with the path, let's walk on the other side of the fence."

Indeed, when they climbed over the stile they could see a path running along the fence on the soft grass of the meadow. "Just as I thought!" said CHRISTIAN. "This is much easier going. Hop over, HOPEFUL."

HOPEFUL was dubious. "Suppose it leads us out of our way?" he asked.

"Unlikely," said CHRISTIAN. "Look, you can see it runs alongside the main path." So HOPEFUL climbed over the stile, and they found the parallel path much easier on their feet.

Suddenly there was a 'ting ting' and up behind them came a cyclist (whose name was VAIN-CONFIDENCE). The Pilgrims offered him some of their water. He stopped, got off his bike, and gratefully took a swig from HOPEFUL's flask.

"Where does this path lead?" asked HOPEFUL.

The cyclist answered: "To the Celestial Gate."

"I told you so," said CHRISTIAN.

The cyclist remounted his bike, waved goodbye, and headed off into the distance. The Pilgrims trudged onwards as it began to get dark.

Night fell quickly, it grew very dark indeed, and they could not see the cyclist ahead of them. VAIN-CONFIDENCE was pedalling along the path when he suddenly went over the edge of a large pit which the landowner had dug to catch trespassers, poachers and *vain-glorious fools withal.*

CHRISTIAN and HOPEFUL heard the crash as he went into the abyss, and ran ahead to find out what had happened. They shouted out, but all they could hear was a groaning.

HOPEFUL said rather quietly, "Where are we now?"

CHRISTIAN stood silent, realising that he had led HOPEFUL astray.

It began to rain, and then to thunder, as flashes of forked lightning streaked across the sky. The path could not take the stormwater, and the water level around them began to rise.

*Then HOPEFUL groaned in himself, saying, "Oh that I had kept on my way!"*

CHRISTIAN huddled under a tree, and tried to keep the rain out of his eyes. He shook his head: "Who would have thought this path would lead us astray?"

"I was worried when we climbed over the stile, which is why I asked the question," said HOPEFUL, miserably. "I wanted to be more forceful, but you are older than I am."

"*Good brother*, forgive me," said CHRISTIAN, "this is all my fault. I am so sorry that I have brought you into such danger. I have been stupid, but believe me, I did not do this with any *evil intent."*

"Don't worry, of course I forgive you," said HOPEFUL. "I do think all this will be for our good."

CHRISTIAN stepped out on to the path, looking back the way they had come. Murky floodwater was pouring down the track.

"You are very forbearing," he said. "I do not deserve that. But we can't stay here, so let's try and retrace our steps to the stile."

"I'll lead the way," said HOPEFUL.

"No," said CHRISTIAN, "let me go first so that if there is any danger, I will be the one to cop it. I am the one to blame, so I must be the one to take the risks."

HOPEFUL restrained CHRISTIAN with his hand. "You are too distressed by all of this. I don't think you're in the right frame of mind to lead the way." *Then, for their encouragement, they heard the voice of one saying, "Set thine heart toward the highway, even the way that thou wentest; turn again".*

The waters were rising fast, and the way back to the stile looked very dangerous. (It struck me as I watched them that it is easier to leave the road when you are on it, then to get back on to it when you have left it.) But the Pilgrims set off, clinging on to each other for safety; it was so dark, and the flood was so high, they reckoned they came close to drowning nine or ten times.

In spite of all their efforts, they could not get back to the stile that night. Finding a wall beside some thick bushes, they huddled together out of the wind to wait for the dawn. Worn out, they soon fell asleep.

But unknown to them, in the dark they had wandered on to the estate of Doubting Castle.

# 28 DOUBTING CASTLE

Early the next morning, the landowner GIANT DESPAIR was walking his dogs and found the two men sound asleep.

He kicked them both and they awoke to find themselves face to face with two slavering Rottweilers and, towering over them, an enormous man.

"And what do you think you're doing here?" he said, *with a grim and surly voice*. They told him that they were Pilgrims who had lost their way.

"Hah, you're trespassing," grunted the giant. "I know your sort, breaking into property and trampling the crops. Come with me."

Unwillingly, the Pilgrims stood up. GIANT DESPAIR lifted them by their collars and shoved and pushed them off down a track, followed by the dogs, baring their teeth. There was not much CHRISTIAN and HOPEFUL could say, as they knew they were in the wrong.

When they reached the castle, the GIANT DESPAIR opened a door in the courtyard, dragged them along a corridor and pushed them down some stairs into a stinking dungeon. Their spirits sank as the darkness closed around them.

Without food or water, they lay alone in the blackness *from Wednesday morning till Saturday night.* They longed to see a friendly face, and CHRISTIAN was doubly distressed, because he knew it was all his fault.

Now GIANT DESPAIR's wife was a suspicious, mistrustful giantess called DIFFIDENCE. In bed that night, GIANT DESPAIR told her he had caught two trespassers and imprisoned them in the dungeon. He asked her what he should do with them.

"Who are they? Where have they come from? Where do they say they're going? We don't want any of these Pilgrims on our land. If you ask me you should give them a good beating," she said.

So next morning, instead of doing his thirty minutes on the rowing machine, the giant went down into the dungeon with his favourite cudgel, made of knobbly crab-tree wood and guaranteed to hurt.

He cursed and swore at the Pilgrims as if they were foxes after his chickens, but the two men said nothing. In a rage, he beat them senseless, and stormed back up the stairs. The Pilgrims gradually regained consciousness and for the rest of the day *spent the time in nothing but sighs and bitter lamentations.*

In bed the next night, the giantess was disappointed to hear that the Pilgrims were still alive. "That's not good enough," she said.

"I beat them as hard as I could and they won't die," grumbled her husband.

"Well, why not make them top themselves?" suggested the giantess.

So in the morning, GIANT DESPAIR went down to the dungeon. CHRISTIAN and HOPEFUL were weak and aching from the vicious blows he had given them the day before.

"You realise I'm never going to let you out," the giant gloated. His harsh voice and cruel tone made them feel worse.

"Your best bet is to make an end of yourselves," he said. "I can let you have a knife, a rope or some poison. Why choose life when it will be unbearable?*"*

The Pilgrims begged him to let them go, but that only made him angry, and he picked up his club. But as he rushed towards the Pilgrims, who thought death was seconds away, he staggered and clutched his chest; he had a medical condition, and sometimes in hot weather he *fell into fits* and temporarily lost the use of his hand. Dropping his club, he limped back up the stairs holding his chest.

The two prisoners sat in the darkness.

CHRISTIAN said quietly: "My brother, what are we going to do? This is a miserable existence: is it better to go on living like this, or to take our own lives? I think the grave may be better than this dungeon. Can we allow despair to dominate our lives? *Shall we be ruled by the Giant?"*

HOPEFUL groaned as he tried to sit up. "This is awful," he said, "and I, too, have been feeling that I'd rather die than suffer here any longer, but *the Lord of the country to which we are going* has said, 'You must not commit murder', and that includes killing yourself. Killing someone else is an offence against the body, but suicide is an offence against the body and the soul. You talk as if death would bring relief, but have you not forgotten the *Hell, whither for certain the murderers go?*

"In any case," HOPEFUL went on, "GIANT DESPAIR is not all-powerful. I've heard of others who have been captured by him and have escaped. *Who knows but that God that made the world may cause that GIANT DESPAIR may die?* Or he may forget to lock the door, or he might have another fit and become completely helpless?

"If that ever happens again, I am determined to escape. I am really stupid for not having tried before, but come on, my brother, let us wait patiently for a bit longer. Some opportunity may come along; *but let us not be our own murderers."*

HOPEFUL started to think of all sorts of escape-from-Colditz-style scenarios. "Have we got a teaspoon? We could dig our way out with that," he suggested.

They didn't, but CHRISTIAN began to cheer up. For the rest of the day they talked quietly in the dark*, in their sad and doleful condition.*

As evening darkened, GIANT DESPAIR came down into the dungeon to see if the prisoners had taken his advice. Shining a torch on to them, he saw them gaze feebly back at him. Starved and beaten, they were barely alive, and could do little more than breathe.

The giant flew into a rage. "If you won't end your miserable lives, I'll make you wish you had never been born," he yelled as he stormed out.

At this point CHRISTIAN passed out. When he came round, it seemed to him they had reached the end of the line. "Surely we would do better to kill ourselves, like the giant said," he murmured.

But HOPEFUL painfully sat up and said: "Wait – think back over all you have been through on your journey so far, how brave you have been and how desperate some of the situations were that you have been through. APOLLYON could not get the better of you. You made it through all the horrors of the Valley of the Shadow of Death. You've seen it all – hardship and terror – so why have you gone to pieces now?

"I am not as strong in my faith as you are," HOPEFUL went on, "and I have been beaten up just as you have, but I know we have to hang in there."

HOPEFUL was insistent. "We are in this together and we will get out together. *Remember how thou playedst the man at Vanity*

*Fair,* and laughed at the threat of imprisonment, and even the risk of martyrdom! We can cope with this. If nothing else, we can bear it with strength and dignity as followers of Jesus, and not shame ourselves."

That night, as GIANT DESPAIR climbed into bed, his wife looked coyly at him from under her curlers, and as they snuggled up together she asked if the prisoners were dead. "Not yet," said the giant, unbuttoning her flannel nightie, "they are *sturdy rogues* and prefer to suffer rather than die."

The giantess put her finger on his lips and said: "Then tomorrow you must take them into the courtyard and show them the bones and skulls of some of our previous Pilgrim visitors. Tell them that they have one week left to live before you start to get a bit rough with them, like you did with the others." They both giggled at the prospect.

There was a red tinge to the dawn sky when the giant went down into the dungeon and hoisted a weakened Pilgrim under each arm. He took them out to the courtyard, where they blinked in the daylight. He dumped them on the flagstones and pointed to a pile of bones against one wall.

"Those," he said, "are the remains of Pilgrims who have trespassed on my land. When I get really mad, I can tear people into pieces like rag dolls. At some stage in the next ten days I am sure I will get really really mad." Then, lifting each Pilgrim by the scruff of the neck, he goose-stepped back to the dungeon entrance, arms out stretched, kicking each one alternately.

It was now Saturday, and the Pilgrims lay all day bruised and semi-conscious on the damp floor of the dungeon.

# 29 WITH ONE BOUND THEY WERE FREE

That evening, the giantess found her husband was in a bad mood. "Those wretches are still alive!" he spat. "Why don't they just give up?"

"I wonder if they have some secret hope that they will be rescued," his wife suggested.

She scratched her nose thoughtfully. "Perhaps they have some hidden tool with which they think they can pick the lock?"

The giant was alert. "Do you really think that's possible?" he asked. "I'll go and search them right away."

"In the morning, dearest," said his wife, oozing over to him. "I've got a surprise for you now..."

And she took off her dressing gown to reveal some exotic underwear (sixe XXXXL) she had discovered at the local Ann Summers. The old giant forgot about the Pilgrims and chased her into the bedroom.

About midnight the cold air revived the Pilgrims in the dungeon. They began to pray, and continued to pray until the first grey light of Sunday morning crept under the door at the top of the stairs.

"I don't believe it," said CHRISTIAN, suddenly. "What an absolute fool I am. I have been lying in this stinking dungeon when I've had the means to escape with me all along."

He rummaged around in the many pockets of the jacket he had been given at the Cross, and pulled out a key.

"Look .. at .. this!" he shouted, jumping up and down and waving it in the air. "What an idiot, what a twit head, what an absolute clot, what a complete imbecile, what a …"

HOPEFUL struggled to his feet, "Yes, yes, my brother, but why do you think this key will work?"

"Because this is the key called PROMISE," shouted CHRISTIAN, "and I am convinced it will open any lock in Doubting Castle!"

He was now dancing around the dungeon like a whirling dervish.

"Right, well, that sounds good," said HOPEFUL, hesitantly, "but would you mind actually trying it in the lock of the dungeon door first?"

CHRISTIAN stopped, looked at HOPEFUL, and then limped stiffly up the stairs to the door. He put the key in the lock, and as he turned it the bolt slid back and the door *flew open with ease.*

CHRISTIAN and HOPEFUL hobbled out of their dungeon. They went along the corridor that led to the door into the courtyard, and found that the key opened this door as well.

The Pilgrims walked out into the dawn of Sunday and headed across the courtyard to the iron gate that led to the outside world. This lock was very stiff, but with some experimenting they found the right way to use the key to prise back the mechanism.

They slowly pushed the gate open. It was very rusty and made a loud grating noise as it moved.

This woke GIANT DESPAIR, who leapt out of bed, looked out of the window, and then rushed to the ornate baronial staircase down to the Grand Hall, to head off the prisoners from the front entrance.

As he leapt two steps at a time past the carved griffins, eagles and lions, he felt the pain rising in his chest, and as he came to the bottom of the staircase he had another of his fits, his limbs failed completely, and he collapsed in a heap on the Tyrannosaurus skin rug at the bottom.

The Pilgrims ran down the drive, back over the field to the stile, and at last came to the *King's highway* again where they were safe, beyond the reach of GIANT DESPAIR.

From the road they stood looking at the stile, and wondered what they could do to warn other Pilgrims. They decided to put up a notice, and using the Swiss Army Knife that CHRISTIAN had found in another pocket, they engraved on an old piece of fencing they found beside the road:

> *'Over this stile is the way to Doubting Castle; which is kept by* GIANT DESPAIR, *who despiseth the King of the Celestial Country, and seeks to destroy the holy pilgrims.'*

Many future Pilgrims had good reason to be grateful to CHRISTIAN and HOPEFUL for this warning.

They walked on in silence for several miles, and coming to a village Post Office they went in and bought some sandwiches and drinks.

"I've thought of some new words to that tune you wrote," said CHRISTIAN:

*'Out of the way we went; and then we found*
*What 'twas to tread upon forbidden ground:*
*And let them that come after have a care,*
*Lest heedlessness makes them, as we to fare;*

*Lest they, for trespassing, his prisoners are,*
*Whose Castle's 'Doubting' and whose name's Despair.'*

The two Pilgrims journeyed on, and eventually arrived at the Delectable Mountains, which CHRISTIAN had seen in the distance from Palace Beautiful.

The slopes were covered with gardens, orchards and vineyards, while clear streams of water gurgled down the hillside. They helped themselves to fruit and refreshed themselves by washing in the streams.

As they went to drink from a fountain, a sheepdog bounded towards them, and along the path came a group of men in rather battered Barbour jackets and Wellingtons.

## TIME FOR A COFFEE BREAK

What would you be prepared to die for?

If consumers do not consume, the economy cannot grow. By refusing to buy, the Pilgrims are effectively taking a stand against the idea of growth as the prime economic objective of the community. Should Christians today do the same?

One person's freedom fighter is another person's terrorist: are there limits on how we deal with injustice or campaign against it?

What is the biggest moral dilemma you face or have faced in the workplace? How do you or did you handle it?

What role should the Church have in helping people cope with pressures in the workplace?

Is an ambition to amass wealth to finance the work of the Kingdom of God an ambition that is acceptable to God?

Should we pray that God will give us financial prosperity?

How do you deal with doubts about yourself and your ability to cope with what life throws at you?

If you know somebody who believed, but now is not so sure, how would you try and help them?

In what sense are doubts healthy?

The Puritans were not known for their sense of humour. Is laughter part of a healthy Christian discipleship?

# 30 THE DELECTABLE MOUNTAINS

One of the men was carrying a crook and he whistled to the dog, who raced up the hill to head off some sheep that had wandered into a garden and started to browse an attractive display of Begonias.

The Pilgrims went to talk to the Shepherds; *and, leaning upon their staves (as is common with weary Pilgrims when they stand to talk with any by the way), they asked,* "Who owns this land and these sheep?"

*"These mountains are Immanuel's Land, and they are within sight of his City; and the sheep also are his, and he laid down his life for them,"* said one of the Shepherds.

"Are we on the right road for the Celestial City?" asked CHRISTIAN.

"You are indeed," said the Shepherd with the crook.

"How far is it now to the City?" asked CHRISTIAN.

*"Too far for any but those that shall get thither indeed,"* was the rather cryptic reply.

"Is it a safe road?" asked CHRISTIAN.

Another enigmatic response: *"Safe for those for whom it is to be safe; but transgressors shall fall therein."*

“Ah, right,” said CHRISTIAN. “And are we allowed to rest here?”

This time the Shepherd was more reassuring.

“The Lord of these mountains is very keen that we should be hospitable to strangers, so make yourselves at home,” he said. “But tell us about yourselves: where are you from, and how has your journey been so far? What kept you persevering on the way?”

The Shepherds led them over to the fountain, and they all sat down. CHRISTIAN started to tell his story, while HOPEFUL added his adventures, and reminded CHRISTIAN of some of the important encounters.

The oldest Shepherd pulled out a hip flask, took a swig and passed it to HOPEFUL, who hesitated, took a sip, spluttered and went bright red.

At this the Shepherds’ weather-beaten faces creased into a smile for the first time. “Welcome to the Delectable Mountains,” said one of the men. “I am afraid that few people who start out on the journey to come here, do actually show their face on these mountains.”

The Shepherds introduced themselves as KNOWLEDGE, EXPERIENCE, WATCHFUL and SINCERE. They invited the Pilgrims back to their farmhouse for supper.

“Stay with us for a bit,” said SINCERE. “We can have a good talk and you ought to have some rest and enjoy the good things of these Mountains.” By this time it was late and CHRISTIAN and HOPEFUL were glad to accept a bed for the night.

The next morning, after an enormous breakfast, the Pilgrims and Shepherds want for a walk through the mountains, appreciating the magnificent landscape.

*"Shall we show these pilgrims some wonders?"* asked EXPERIENCE.

"Why not?" replied KNOWLEDGE. "Let's take them for a walk up Crib Goch and along the knife-edge."

They later found themselves walking along a narrow track along the top of a ridge. The land fell away steeply on both sides, but precipitously on the left. Looking down, CHRISTIAN and HOPEFUL saw at the bottom the bodies of several people who had fallen off.

"This is a dangerous place!" said HOPEFUL, nervously.

"Dead right," said WATCHFUL.

"This is the Ridge of Error," said KNOWLEDGE. "Those bodies are of pilgrims who were led astray by theologians whose eschatology was wrong."

"Their what?" asked HOPEFUL.

"2 Timothy 2:17-18," replied KNOWLEDGE. "They went wrong by listening to *Hymenius and Philetus, as concerning the faith of the Resurrection of the body.* Doctrinal truth does matter, because wrong doctrine can destroy faith. We have left them unburied as a warning to others *to take heed how they clamber too high, or how they come too near the brink of this mountain."*

They continued along the sharp ridge, and came to another summit, called Caution Peak. The Shepherds pointed down into the valley where there appeared to be men stumbling around among tombs.

Looking through the Shepherds' binoculars, the Pilgrims could see that these men were blind; they kept falling over as they stretched out their hands to feel the tombstones, attempting to grope their way out of the graveyard.

“What’s going on down there?” asked CHRISTIAN.

“They were Pilgrims, just like you,” he was told. “Did you notice as we came up the first ridge that there was a stile on the left, leading into a meadow? Over that stile the path takes you directly to Doubting Castle and GIANT DESPAIR. When those Pilgrims down there came to the stile, they saw the way ahead was rough, so they climbed over the stile for the easier walk in the meadow.

“They were caught by GIANT DESPAIR and thrown in the dungeons of Doubting Castle. After a time in there, the giant put out their eyes, and abandoned them among those tombs, where they wander to this day. This is exactly what the wise old writer said in Proverbs 21:16: **’The man that wandereth out of the way of understanding shall remain in the congregation of the dead’**.”

CHRISTIAN and HOPEFUL looked at each other in horror, but said nothing to the Shepherds.

*Then I saw in my dream* that the Shepherds led them down a steep slope to the bottom of a valley. Among some rocks was a door into the side of the hill. The Shepherds opened the door and told them to look inside. CHRISTIAN and HOPEFUL peered into a dark and smoky cave. They thought they heard a rumbling noise like flames, mingled with tormented cries, and they smelt the stench of brimstone.

“What does this mean?” asked CHRISTIAN.

The Shepherds told them: *“This is a byway to hell, a way that hypocrites go in at:* people like Esau who sold his birthright, or Judas who sold his Master; people like Alexander who *blaspheme the Gospel,* or those like Ananias and Sapphira who lie and deceive.*”*

HOPEFUL said to the Shepherds: “All of these were on a pilgrimage, just like us, weren’t they?”

"Yes," said the Shepherds, "and they followed the road for some time, too."

"How far did they get on their pilgrimage, even though they ended up cast into the pit?" asked HOPEFUL.

"Some got further than these mountains, and some not so far," was the oblique reply.

The Pilgrims looked at each other, and said: *"We had need to cry to the strong for strength."*

"Aye," said the Shepherds, "and you will need to use your strength when you have it, too."

The Pilgrims were now ready to move on. The Shepherds agreed, and so walked with them towards the end of the mountain range.

"We should show the Pilgrims the gates of the Celestial City," said one of the Shepherds. "They might get a glimpse through our binoculars."

The Pilgrims were keen to try, and climbed a high hill named Clear. But when they looked through the binoculars, the memory of the door in the hillside made their hands shake so much that they could see little more than a blur. *Yet they thought they saw something like the gate, and also some of the glory of the place.*

Walking back down the hill, they thought of Iona, and the memory of their time on the island brought a tune back. They put some new words to it:

*'Thus by the Shepherds secrets are revealed,*
*Which from all other men are kept concealed:*
*Come to the Shepherds, then, if you would see*
*Things deep, things hid, and that mysterious be.'*

As they were saying their farewells, one Shepherd gave them an Ordnance Survey map.

Another told them: “Beware of the Flatterer.”

The third warned them not to sleep on the ‘Enchanted Ground’, and the fourth simply wished them Godspeed.

*So I awoke from my dream.*

# 31 THE MUGGING OF LITTLE-FAITH

*And I slept, and dreamed again; and saw the same two Pilgrims going down the mountains, along the High-way towards the City.* The Shepherd's map was useful, and they kept a look out for anybody who looked like the 'Flatterer', while watching out for any signs that might identify the Enchanted Ground.

At the foot of the mountains, off towards the left, lay Conceit County. A little crooked lane led from this part of the world to the Pilgrims' road.

Striding down this lane came a self-confident young man in a double-breasted suit, whose name was IGNORANCE. CHRISTIAN greeted him, and asked him where he had come from, and where he was going.

"Hi," said IGNORANCE. "I grew up in Conceit, up the lane there, and I am going to the Celestial City."

"But how are you going to get in? Won't that be a difficulty?" asked CHRISTIAN.

"Why on earth should it be?" He sounded surprised, and raised an eyebrow at CHRISTIAN. "I will get in like any other good person, for heaven's sake."

"But what have you got to show at the gate?" persisted CHRISTIAN.

*"I know my Lord's will,* and I have led a good life*: I pay every man his own; I pray, fast, pay tithes, and give alms, and have left my country for whither I am going,"* said IGNORANCE.

"Yes, but you did not come in at the wicket gate at the beginning of this road," insisted CHRISTIAN. "You have joined us from this winding lane, and I fear you won't get into the City because you will be accused of being a thief and a robber, and they won't admit you."

"Look, mate," said IGNORANCE, "I don't know who you are, but you follow your religion, and I'll follow mine. I am sure everything will be all right on the night, and as for the wicket gate you talk about, everyone knows it is miles back from where we are now.

"In fact, I'd bet my bonus that my mates stand as much chance of finding the gate as finding a bacon buttie at a Bar Mitzvah. It really doesn't matter if they find it or not, anyway, as we have our own perfectly nice little lane on to this road."

CHRISTIAN *saw that the man was wise in his own conceit*, so he whispered to HOPEFUL: "This man is a fool in a Proverbs and Ecclesiastes sense of the word, and I am afraid this is going to be evident to anyone as soon as he opens his mouth. Should we talk to him now or wait until later when he has had time to think, and see if we can gradually help him?"

HOPEFUL whistled the tune of a song he knew CHRISTIAN would recognise:

*"Let IGNORANCE a little while now muse*
*On what is said; and let him not refuse*
*Good counsel to embrace, lest he remain*
*Still ignorant of what's the chiefest gain.*
*God saith 'Those that no understanding have*
*(Although he made them) them he will not save'."*

HOPEFUL added: "We are not going to be able to tell him everything all at once. Let's talk to him later."

IGNORANCE had stopped for a smoke, so the Pilgrims pressed on down the road until they came to *a very dark lane; where they met a man whom seven devils had bound with seven strong cords, and were carrying of him back to the door that they saw in the side of the hill.*

CHRISTIAN and HOPEFUL looked on in horror, and wondered whom the poor man might be. CHRISTIAN thought it might be someone he knew called TURN-AWAY, who lived in the Town of Apostasy. The man was hiding his face like a thief who has just been caught, but HOPEFUL spotted a note pinned to his back: *'Wanton professor, and damnable apostate.'*

The two Pilgrims walked on, speeding up their pace rather anxiously. In the distance they could see smoke billowing out of a factory chimney, and as they came closer they could see that there was a large crowd camped outside the factory gate.

A car overtook the Pilgrims and approached the factory, and the crowd went wild, waving placards and shouting abuse. A number of them hammered on the car roof, but it pushed on slowly and firmly. An army of security guards opened the gate and shepherded the car in.

"What's going on?" HOPEFUL asked a woman holding a baby.

"My husband's just been made redundant, with a whole load of others," she told him. "We are fed up with the ruthless behaviour of the management, let alone the pollution this factory produces. They do nothing! They say the recession is killing their markets, and they can't borrow money to invest."

"Times are difficult," said CHRISTIAN. "I know it is not easy running a business."

"But the bosses look after themselves, don't they?" said an angry student. "That bloke in the Skoda who drove in is the Managing

Director. We know he still has his Bentley, and that Skoda wasn't even his wife's, it was the au pair's!"

HOPEFUL said: "Er, right, well we are really sorry. We'll stay with you for a bit and join the protest, if that would help."

"Thanks, guys, here's a couple of placards to wave. I hear the MP is supposed to be coming along soon to see for herself."

CHRISTIAN and HOPEFUL stood rather self-consciously beside the road.

"Seeing that incident earlier reminds me of a chap who lived near here," CHRISTIAN said after a while. "His name was LITTLE-FAITH. He really was a good man, from the Town of Sincere."

"Go on," said HOPEFUL, "tell me the story."

CHRISTIAN dug back in his memory. "Back there was Deadman's Lane, which comes down from Broadway Gate; it gets its name from the number of murders and muggings that have happened there. LITTLE-FAITH was a pilgrim like us. He stopped there for a nap and it so happened he was on the corner of Deadman's Lane.

"Unluckily for him, three local yobs, brothers called FAINT-HEART, MISTRUST, and GUILT, came down the lane and spotted him. As he woke up he found these three hoodies bearing down on him. LITTLE-FAITH went white as a sheet and froze.

"'Giv' us yer money,' said FAINT-HEART, but LITTLE-FAITH was too petrified to move. MISTRUST grabbed him by the jacket and found his wallet.

"'Thieves! Thieves!' shouted LITTLE-FAITH, but GUILT hit him on the head with a bicycle chain, and he fell to the ground bleeding profusely. The gang stood around joking for a bit, but hearing someone coming along the road, they ran off. They were afraid that it might be GREAT-GRACE from the City of Good-Confidence, so they scarpered and left LITTLE-FAITH in the gutter.

"LITTLE-FAITH regained consciousness after a while, picked himself up and went on his way."

"So did he lose everything he had?" asked HOPEFUL.

"No," said CHRISTIAN, "he had hidden his Credit Card in his shoe, so they did not find it. But he was very distressed by the loss of his spending money, and had to survive on the small change in his back pocket for the rest of his journey. In fact, I believe he was forced to beg to keep himself alive."

"It was a good thing they didn't get his Roll, his entrance certificate for the Celestial Gate."

"I think it was more by good luck than by any good judgment on his part," replied CHRISTIAN.

"And it must have been a comfort to him that he still had his Credit Card."

"Well it would have been if he had used it," said CHRISTIAN, "but those who told me the story said that he was so upset by the loss of his wallet that he scarcely used it at all. Whenever he thought of it, he was overcome by the memory of the loss of his wallet; so instead of using what he did have, he agonised and grieved about what he did not have."

"Poor bloke," said HOPEFUL.

"Yes indeed," said CHRISTIAN, "and I expect any of us would have felt the same way if we had been beaten up, robbed and left for dead in a strange place. It was surprising he didn't die of shock. Apparently, he spent the rest of his journey telling everyone he met the sorry tale of how he was mugged, who did it, what was taken, what his wounds were, how lucky he was to be alive at all, and how awful the whole thing had been."

"But I still don't understand why he didn't use his Credit Card to cover his needs on the journey."

"Don't be so thick," said CHRISTIAN. "He couldn't sell or pawn his Card, and actually he didn't really want to use it. In any case, without his Credit Card at the *gate of the Celestial City* he knew he would be *excluded from an inheritance there*; that would have been worse than a million lost wallets."

"There is no need to be rude," said HOPEFUL. "Esau sold out his birthright for a bowl of stew, so why not LITTLE-FAITH?"

"They are not the same," responded CHRISTIAN. "Many people like Esau fail to recognise what has real value, and so deprive themselves of a great blessing. But cowardly Esau and LITTLE-FAITH are different personalities and in different positions. Esau's 'birthright' in the Old Testament was a symbol of something greater. But LITTLE-FAITH'S Credit Card is real – it is the actual faith that he has, however small.

"*Esau's belly was his God*, his desire was his bodily appetite. This was not the case with LITTLE-FAITH. Esau could see no further than satisfying his own lusts. 'I'm dying,' he said, 'so what's the point of keeping my birthright?' But LITTLE-FAITH, *was by his little faith kept from such extravagances*, and his faith prevented him from throwing away his Credit Card."

CHRISTIAN took out his water bottle and took a swig. "It does not say anywhere that Esau had any faith at all. So where there is no faith to restrain the lusts of the flesh, it is no surprise if a man sells his birthright, his soul, his everything to the devil. Such a man is no better than a donkey. People who are driven by lusts are not concerned about the cost."

He offered some water to the woman with the baby, but she smiled and shook her head.

"But LITTLE-FAITH was different," continued CHRISTIAN, "his mind was actually on higher things. He really did care about the spiritual side of life, so why should somebody like that get rid of his Credit Card? Even if somebody had been willing to buy it, why would he want to *fill his mind with empty things?* Would anyone pay money just to eat hay? It was not in his nature. Could you persuade a turtledove to live off carrion, like a crow?

"Even though people without any faith will pawn, mortgage or sell their possessions and even themselves to satisfy their lusts, a person with faith, *saving faith*, however little, simply cannot do this. That's where you're wrong, my brother."

"I suppose so," said HOPEFUL, "but I find your rudeness very irritating."

"I only said you were thick!" said CHRISTIAN. "But I really am sorry for upsetting you. Please think of it as the rough and tumble of debate, and don't let's fall out over it."

"Alright," said HOPEFUL, "I forgive you, but let's hope this MP comes along soon, I want to get moving again."

They stood in silence for a bit, holding their placards.

"But CHRISTIAN, those hoodies were just a bunch of cowards. They ran away at the sound of somebody coming down the road, so why didn't LITTLE-FAITH show more guts? He could have had a go at them and only handed over his wallet when he really had no alternative."

"It's easy to think that all muggers are really cowards at heart," pointed out CHRISTIAN, "but it is hard to feel that confident when they come to attack you, and you don't know if they have knives up their sleeves. LITTLE-FAITH was not known for his great courage.

"If you had been in his position, HOPEFUL, I'm sure you would indeed have gone on the attack, but that is easy to say at this distance. Even you might have second thoughts if they suddenly came round the corner now. And remember, these are only ordinary gang members – the gang leader is *the king of the bottomless pit*. When necessary, he will come himself to help out his thugs, and he is a terrifying adversary."

Nothing seemed to be happening with the protest. No MP had turned up, and one or two people had started to walk off. A couple with a tent had begun to cook a meal.

"I think I am beginning to have little faith in the effectiveness of this protest as a way of achieving anything," said CHRISTIAN.

"It is very important to make a stand against injustice," said HOPEFUL, "but you may have a point. Let's quietly continue on our way."

CHRISTIAN was silent for a bit. Then they handed back the placards to the protesters who had lent them, wished them well, and set off again along the road, each deep in his own thoughts.

Then CHRISTIAN said: "I once had an experience just like LITTLE-FAITH's, and it was awful."

# 32 BE PREPARED

HOPEFUL waited for a bit and then asked: "So what happened?"

CHRISTIAN was obviously finding it difficult to talk about it, so his friend let him take his time.

At last he said: "Three thugs tried to grab my mobile phone and, *I beginning like a Christian to resist,* they shouted for help and this big bruiser came out of a doorway. At that point I wouldn't have given a peanut for my chances, but, *as God would have it, I was clothed with Armour of Proof.* Even so, it was hard work to hold my own, and if you have never been in the thick of a battle, you can have no idea of what it is really like."

"But LITTLE-FAITH's attackers did run when they thought GREAT-GRACE was coming round the corner," said HOPEFUL.

"True," said CHRISTIAN, "but GREAT-GRACE is the King's champion. All he has to do is walk in, and gangs and their leaders simply vanish. But it is unfair to compare LITTLE-FAITH and the King's champion; not all the King's subjects are his champions, nor can they do what he does.

"Is it right to think that any child could have handled Goliath like David did? Or that a wren should be as strong as an ox? *Some are strong, some are weak; some have great faith, some have little: this man was one of the weak; and therefore he went to the wall."*

"I wish it had been GREAT-GRACE coming along the road," said

HOPEFUL. "He would have sorted the hoodies out."

"He might have had his hands full," said CHRISTIAN. "Although GREAT-GRACE is superb in armed combat, if someone like FAINT-HEART or MISTRUST can get in at close range, they can floor him. And when a man is down, what can he do?

"The scars and cuts on GREAT-GRACE's face tell their own story. It is said that on one occasion in a fight he said: *"We despaired even of life*."

"How was it that attackers made *David groan, moan, and roar?* Even *Heman and Hezekiah,* though champions in their day, had a tough time.

"Peter was always ready to take on the Lord's enemies, but even though he is *the Prince of the Apostles*, he ended up being afraid of a slip of a girl.

"All the thugs have to do is whistle, and their leader, if he can, will come running to help. He is incredibly tough, just look at Job 41. So what can you do? If you had Job's horse, with its skill and courage, as in Job 39, you might acquit yourself like a hero.

"But for ordinary people like you and me, let's hope we never get into a fight, nor think that we would have done better when we hear of the failure of others, *nor be tickled at the thoughts of our own manhood,* for such pride often leads to a fall.

"Remember Peter again: he boasted he would never let his master down, but he failed miserably when challenged.

"So when we hear of these attacks on the King's highway, we should remember two things: first, go out *harnessed,* and second, as the expert taught us, 'always carry your shield of faith'. Without faith, *Leviathan* will not be defeated. Indeed, he has no fear of someone without faith.

"Actually, it is a good idea to ask the King for someone to accompany us – in fact, that he himself should go with us. This thought comforted David in *the Valley of the Shadow of Death*; and in Exodus 33 Moses preferred to die where he stood *than to go one step without his God*.

"So, my brother, if he comes with us, why should we be afraid of ten thousand attackers? *But without him, the proud helpers fall under the slain*, as Isaiah 10 tells us.

"Through God's goodness, I have been through the mill and survived. But I won't go in for any macho boasting. I shall be glad if there are no more skirmishes, though I fear we are not out of danger yet.

"However, since the lion and the bear have not yet got me, *I hope God will also deliver us from the next uncircumcised Philistine."*

CHRISTIAN paused. "That song you whistled earlier," he said, "I remember a bit of another verse:

*"Poor LITTLE-FAITH! hast been among the thieves?*
*Wast robbed? Remember this: whoso believes,*
*And gets more faith, shall then a victor be*
*Over ten thousand, else scarce over three."*

Behind them, the Pilgrims spotted IGNORANCE following at a distance, and looking ahead they could see that they were approaching the suburbs of a small town.

Through the traffic that was building up, they could see a fork in the road ahead. However, both roads seemed to run close together, and it was difficult to see which one to take: they both looked equally straight.

They stopped by the traffic lights at the junction and, looking around, saw a small group of people talking animatedly. The centre of attention seemed to be a man in civic robes, whom CHRISTIAN presumed to be one of the local town councillors.

Seeing CHRISTIAN and HOPEFUL looking a bit lost, the Councillor closed the discussion, cracked a joke, and said goodbye to the group. He walked over to the Pilgrims who were hesitating at the lights, and asked them why they had stopped?

They looked at him: his appearance was slightly odd. His smile didn't seem quite genuine, but he was very well spoken, obviously Public School, probably a Conservative.

They heard later that he actually went to the old town Grammar School, and was an Independent as none of the parties would have him.

His fur-trimmed robes and glittering gold chain were so magnificent that they felt honoured to be addressed by him, and be welcomed and commended by him for their progress on their journey.

"Which road goes to the Celestial City?" asked CHRISTIAN.

"Follow me!" said the man. "That's where I'm going!"

# 33 SOME TOUGH DISCIPLINE

He set off in front of them, and they followed him along the road, which gradually began to diverge from the direction in which they wanted to be heading.

The terraced houses gave way to a more leafy suburban streetscape, but by now the road was taking them completely in the wrong direction.

The Pilgrims still followed on.

Without any warning, as they walked under a tree, a large net dropped on top of them, and tangled them up.

As they struggled, they looked to their guide for help but, with a laugh, he threw off his councillor's robes, displaying a large rosette on his lapel.

He walked up the path of the nearest house to knock on the door and hand out his leaflets.

The Pilgrims were trapped, and they *lay crying some time*.

CHRISTIAN sat with his head in his hands. "I have really messed up again. I might have guessed what would happen if we started believing things candidates tell us in an election campaign.

"The Shepherds warned us to *beware of the Flatterer*, and I should have been on my guard the minute I saw a local politician.

"Any politician, for that matter. We've come all this way, and I still fall for a con artist. I still believe it when somebody tells me how wonderful I am, and I still ignore the warning signs when they are blindingly obvious in front of me.

"And this is the net trap of Proverbs 29:6."

HOPEFUL groaned and said: "We also forgot the Ordnance Survey map the Shepherds gave us. David got it right in Psalm 17 when he said that God's Word would keep us away from the *paths of the destroyer*."

As they struggled in the net, blaming themselves for their stupidity, they saw coming towards them along the track a *Shining One* carrying a whip. He stopped and looked at the Pilgrim flies struggling in the web.

"What are you doing here?" he asked.

CHRISTIAN and HOPEFUL started a sob story, telling him that they were *poor pilgrims going to Zion*, and had mistakenly followed a politician who claimed to be going in the same direction.

Tapping the whip in his hand, the man said, *"It is FLATTERER, a false apostle, that hath transformed himself into an angel of light".* Taking out a pocket knife, he cut the net and told them to follow him back to the right path.

They walked along in silence, and when they came to the junction, he asked them where they had slept the previous night. They told him they had stayed with the Shepherds on the Delectable Mountains.

"But didn't the Shepherds give you a map?" he asked.

When the Pilgrims admitted that they had, he asked: "So why didn't you use it when you were unsure of the way?"

"We forgot we had it," said the Pilgrims sheepishly.

"And didn't they warn you about the Flatterer?"

There was silence. HOPEFUL looked at CHRISTIAN for help, but CHRISTIAN looked away.

"Yes, they did," said the Pilgrims eventually, "but we had no idea that *this fine spoken man had been he.*"

CHRISTIAN had wondered about the whip, and now his fears were confirmed.

"Lie down on the ground," said the Shining One, rolling up his sleeves.

CHRISTIAN and HOPEFUL knelt down in the road and stretched out face down. The Shining One brought his whip down hard on their backs, and *chastised them sore to teach them the good way wherein they should walk.*

*And as he chastised them, he said: "As many as I love, I rebuke and chasten; be zealous therefore, and repent".*

As the Pilgrims struggled to their feet, he told them to head off down the other track and remember the other directions of the Shepherds.

So they thanked him for his kindness and made their way along the right road, rather gingerly, their backs smarting.

After half a mile, HOPEFUL said: "Time for another verse of that song, I think."

CHRISTIAN groaned, and rather reluctantly joined in:

*"Come hither, you that walk along the way;*
*See how the Pilgrims fare that go astray!*

*They catched are in an entangling net,*
*'Cause they good counsel lightly did forget.*
*'Tis true they rescued were; but yet you see*
*They're scourged to boot. Let this your caution be!"*

The friends travelled on, and after a couple of miles, they saw a lone man coming towards them.

"Here's someone *with his back toward Sion*," said CHRISTIAN.

"I can see that," replied HOPEFUL, "and we had better watch out that he doesn't also try to flatter us."

As the man came nearer, they could see he wore a conference-style badge announcing him to be Dr ATHEIST, a Professor of the Public Understanding of Science. He asked them where they were heading.

"We are going to *the Mount Sion*," said CHRISTIAN, confidently.

Professor ATHEIST fell about laughing.

CHRISTIAN looked offended and asked him what was so funny.

"I am laughing," said ATHEIST, "at your ignorance. All you are going to get for your journey is blisters."

"Why?" asked CHRISTIAN. "Do you think they will not let us in?"

"Let you in!" said ATHEIST. "The place doesn't exist!"

"Maybe not in this world," said HOPEFUL, "but certainly in *the world to come."*

"Colleagues," said the Professor, in the tones of one who lectures for a living. "Trust me. When I was at school I was impressed by the Chaplain, and began to look for the Celestial City. But after more than fifty years of research I have found absolutely nothing."

"We both believe it can be found," replied CHRISTIAN.

"So did I when I started off," said ATHEIST. "And I have been further on the journey than you have, but my extensive investigations have found absolutely nothing. So I am going back to where I started, and I will enjoy all the things I rejected for what I see now was a futile quest."

CHRISTIAN said to HOPEFUL, "Do you think this is true?"

"I think he is just another type of Flatterer," said HOPEFUL, "and remember what it cost us last time. How can you say there is no Mount Sion? Don't you remember we saw the gate of the City from the Delectable Mountains? *Also, are we not now to walk by faith?*

"Come on, let's press on or the man with the whip will overtake us again. Remember Proverbs 19:27: **'Cease, my son, to hear the instruction that causeth thee to err from the words of knowledge'**. Stop listening to such talk, and *let us believe to the saving of the soul."*

"Don't worry," said CHRISTIAN, "I wasn't asking because I doubted the truth of our belief myself, but because I wanted to know what you honestly believe.

"As for this comedian, I know that he is *blinded by the God of this world*: we travel on knowing that we believe the truth; *and no lie is of the truth.*"

HOPEFUL threw his baseball cap in the air, caught it, and high-fived CHRISTIAN.

"*Now do I rejoice in hope of the glory of God!"* he shouted, and did a cartwheel in the road.

ATHEIST, still chuckling to himself, carried on down the road away from them.

*I then saw in my dream* that the road went through a heathland. An aromatic mixture of herbs grew there and as the sun beat down, the air was full of the soothing scents of lavender, valerian and chamomile.

HOPEFUL found he could hardly keep his eyes open, and said to CHRISTIAN, "Look, here is nice little chamomile bed – let's lie down and have a nap."

"We might never wake up," said CHRISTIAN.

"Come on," said HOPEFUL, walking off the road, picking a few flowers as he went. "*Sleep is sweet to the labouring man*. We'll be refreshed after a bit of a zizz."

# 34 THE ENCHANTED GROUND

"Wait," said CHRISTIAN, "didn't one of the Shepherds warn us to beware of the Enchanted Ground? He was warning us about sleeping on the job, like others do. *Let us watch and be sober."*

HOPEFUL stopped, and returned to the road, dropping the stems he had picked.

"Oh glory," he said, "you're right and I'm wrong again. If I had been here on my own, I would probably soon be dead. Just as the wise man of Ecclesiastes said, *'two are better than one'.* You will certainly get a great reward for everything you have done for me."

"Come on," said CHRISTIAN, "we'll have to work hard to prevent drowsiness, so let's keep each other awake by talking."

"Great idea," said HOPEFUL.

"What shall we talk about?"

HOPEFUL thought for a minute and then said: "Let's begin where God began with us. But you first, please."

"OK," said CHRISTIAN. "First I will sing you a song I picked up at Greenbelt:

*'When saints do sleepy grow, let them come hither,*
*And hear how these two Pilgrims talk together;*

*Yea, let them learn of them, in any wise,*
*Thus to keep ope their drowsy, slumbering eyes.*
*Saint's fellowship, if it be managed well,*
*Keeps them awake; and that in spite of hell.'*

CHRISTIAN set a brisk pace, and told HOPEFUL all about his early life in the City of Destruction, his family, his dissatisfaction, and his adventures up to his arrival in Vanity Fair.

"Your turn now," said CHRISTIAN. "Tell me how you started thinking about doing what you are doing now."

"Do you mean why I began to *look after the good of my soul?"*

"Yes, what got you going?"

"I had fun growing up in Vanity Fair, but I now believe that the things I enjoyed there would eventually have *drowned me in perdition and destruction."*

"What sort of things?"

"In a nutshell, *all the treasures and riches of the world*," said HOPEFUL. "I have to say that I liked my nights out with the rugby team, *rioting, revelling, drinking, swearing, lying, uncleanness, Sabbath-breaking* – things that tend to *destroy the soul*.

"But after I began to hear about God, from you and our old friend FAITHFUL, who was martyred in Vanity Fair for his faith and his virtuous life, I came to realise that my supposed pleasures would lead to deadness rather than life. I began to see that they are an offence to God and that *for these things' sake the wrath of God comes upon the children of disobedience."*

"So you were convinced straight away, were you?" asked CHRISTIAN.

"Not at all," said HOPEFUL. "I was not willing even to think about the evil of sin, nor of the consequences of *damnation* that follow the committing of sin. I tried to close my eyes to the light *when my mind at first began to be shaken with the Word*."

"But why were you so resistant *to the first workings of God's blessed Spirit upon you?"* CHRISTIAN asked.

HOPEFUL thought back and tried to analyse his feelings.

Eventually he said: "I would probably put it something like this:

1. In my ignorance, I never realised that God begins the conversion of a sinner by awakening his awareness of sin;

2. Actually, I rather enjoyed sin, and was unwilling to change or leave it behind;

3. I could not think how I could leave my mates, and, in any case, I didn't want to;

4. But when I did think about my sin, I found it unbearably terrifying."

"You did manage to stop thinking about your sin, though?" asked CHRISTIAN.

"Well, yes," said HOPEFUL, "but it would keep coming back into my mind, and then it would be the same, in fact worse, than before."

"What would bring your sins to mind again?"

"Many things," said HOPEFUL, "such as if:

- I met a good man in the street; or,
- I read a verse in the Bible; or,
- I felt unwell; or,
- I heard that some of my neighbours were sick; or,

- I heard the bell toll for someone who had died; or,
- I thought of my own death; or,
- I heard of a sudden death.
- But, particularly, when I thought I myself would soon come to judgment."

"And when this happened, could you easily get rid of your feelings of guilt?"

"No," said HOPEFUL, "after a time these things got a stronger hold on my conscience. So when I was tempted to go back to my old sinful ways – though I had made up my mind not to – it was a double torment for me."

"What did you do?"

"I told myself I had to try harder to mend my ways, or else I would certainly be damned."

"And did you?"

"I did," said HOPEFUL. "I stopped the nights out with my mates, and started going to church. I prayed and read Christian books. I got really worked up about my sins and failures. I dealt honestly with everyone I met. And a lot of other things, too."

"So that was alright then?"

"Yes, for a while; but then my fears came back, in spite of my better behaviour."

"How could that be, since you were a reformed character?"

This was all a bit painful for HOPEFUL, so since they were passing a country churchyard, he bought a gap in the conversation by suggesting they go in and sit in the cool for a bit.

The church was open, and the Pilgrims sat in the pews at the back, and looked at the patterns of light coming in through the stained glass and falling on the ancient stonework.

After a bit of thought, HOPEFUL gave his answer: "A number of things brought it all back, I suppose, but in particular I kept finding verses that unsettled me, like:

> Isaiah 64: 6 **But we are all as an unclean thing, and all our righteousnesses are as filthy rags**;
>
> and Galations 2:16 **For by the works of the law shall no flesh be justified**;
>
> and Luke 17:10 **when ye shall have done all those things which are commanded you, say, `We are unprofitable servants. We have done that which was our duty to do.'**

"I started arguing with myself: if all my righteousness is worthless, it is no good thinking that I will get to Heaven just through abiding by the law.

"I saw it like this: if I run up £1,000 on my credit card one month, but then after that behave sensibly and pay off all my current credit card spending at the end of each month, I still owe MasterCard that £1,000 and they can still sue me for the debt."

CHRISTIAN looked at HOPEFUL: "Probably, but how does this apply?"

"Well," said HOPEFUL, "I thought like this: my sins have run up a huge balance on my Heavenly MasterCard, and all my changed behaviour cannot pay off that particular debt. So I am still liable."

"Yes, good sermon illustration, but go on."

"What also bothered me about my reformed behaviour was that, when I looked at what I did, I could see sin, and new sin, mixed in with my best actions.

“I came to the conclusion that even supposing I had led a faultless life in the past, I was already committing enough sin every day to *send me to hell*.”

“So what did you do then?” asked Christian.

“Do? I had no idea what to do,” admitted his friend.

# 35 FAITHFUL EXPLAINS THE GOOD NEWS

"But then I had an idea," said HOPEFUL.

"I went and talked to FAITHFUL. I had got to know him well by this time, and he told me that *unless I could obtain the righteousness of a Man that never had sinned*, then neither my own goodness nor the goodness of the whole world could save me."

"And do you think he was right?"

"If he had said this to me at the time I was feeling pleased with myself for changing my behaviour, I would have told him he was a fruitcake. But by now I could recognise my weakness and my inability to live a life free of sin, so I found myself compelled to agree with him."

"When he made this suggestion, did you think there actually was anybody who had never committed a sin?" asked CHRISTIAN.

The west window of the church was a fairly typical Victorian composition, with Christ on the cross in the centre, and various characters in side panels. On the left a mediaeval man was holding a rather ugly chalice, surrounded by some venerable elderly women whose pained expressions were probably meant to convey holiness.

HOPEFUL was staring at the window. "I have to admit it did sound odd when he first suggested it, but as I continued to talk to him and spend time with him, it made complete sense to me."

"So did you ask FAITHFUL who this man was, and how *you must be justified by him*?"

"Yes," said HOPEFUL. "*He told me it was the Lord Jesus*, who is at the *right hand of the Most High.* We used to study Hebrews and Romans 4 and Colossians 1 together; and FAITHFUL would tell me that I must be justified by <u>him</u> and trust what <u>he</u> did when he was on earth, and what he suffered on the cross.

"When I asked him how that could justify me before God, FAITHFUL told me that Jesus was *the mighty God* and he lived and died not for himself, but for <u>me</u>; *to whom his doings, and the worthiness of them, should be imputed, if I believed on him."*

"What did you think about that?"

"I argued against such a belief, thinking that Jesus would not be interested in <u>me</u>. FAITHFUL told me to go and ask him, but that sounded so presumptuous. 'Rubbish', said FAITHFUL, 'you have been invited, get on with it – Jesus invites you to come to him'."

HOPEFUL laughed at the memory of his tussles with FAITHFUL, and his reluctance to get going on his journey. "He even gave me a *Book of Jesus* to encourage me. He told me that every word and punctuation mark in the Book *stood firmer than heaven and earth.*

"Eventually I asked him what I should do, and he told me that I should ask God on my knees with all my heart and soul to reveal Jesus to me. I asked him how I should do this, and he told me, *'Go, and thou shalt find him upon a mercy seat, where he sits all the year long to give pardon and forgiveness to them that come'."*

HOPEFUL was staring up at the window again.

"And?" asked CHRISTIAN.

"I told him I didn't know what to say."

After another pause for thought, HOPEFUL pulled out his wallet and took out a scrap of paper. "He had an answer for that, and wrote out this prayer for me:

> *'God be merciful to me a sinner, and make me to know and believe in Jesus Christ; for I see that if his righteousness had not been, or I have not faith in that righteousness, I am utterly cast away. Lord, I have heard that You are a merciful God, and have ordained that Your Son Jesus Christ should be the Saviour of the world: and moreover, that You are willing to bestow him upon such a poor sinner as I am (and I am a sinner indeed); Lord, take therefore this opportunity, and magnify Your grace in the salvation of my soul, through Your Son Jesus Christ. Amen.'*

"And you used that prayer?"

"Yes I did: over, and over, and over again."

"And did the Father reveal the Son to you?"

"No, not when I prayed it the first time, nor the second time, nor the third time, nor the fourth, nor the fifth; nor the sixth time either."

That was not what CHRISTIAN expected to hear, so there was another long silence.

"So," said CHRISTIAN slowly, "what did you do then?"

"I had not the foggiest idea what to do."

"Did you think of stopping praying?"

"Yes, hundreds of times."

"Why didn't you?"

The bell in the clock tower started to toll the hour, and for some reason it relaxed HOPEFUL and he regained some of his usual confidence. "I think because I believed that what he told me was actually true."

He folded his arms and stretched his legs under the pew in front. "The more I thought about it," he said, "the more convinced I became that there was no-one else in the world except the sinless Jesus who could save the sinful me.

"So I reasoned that if I stopped praying, that would be the end, but if it was to be the end anyway, I would rather have the end at the *Throne of Grace*. I came across an obscure verse in Habakkuk 2:3: **'Though it tarry, wait for it, because it will surely come; it will not tarry'**.

"So I just carried on praying, until the Father showed me his Son."

"Just like that?" asked CHRISTIAN.

"Sort of just like that. I did not see anything with my physical eyes, but it was like Paul writes in Ephesians 1 – it was with the *eyes of my understanding.*

"I can remember the day well: I was really down, probably one of the lowest points of my life. I had gone for a walk, and climbed a small hill from where I could look down on Vanity Fair. I was fed up with the meaninglessness and pointlessness of life, and the *greatness and vileness of my sins*. Thoughts of hell, and the everlasting damnation of my soul overwhelmed me…

"But suddenly, *as I thought, I saw the Lord Jesus looking down from heaven upon me, and saying, 'Believe on the Lord Jesus Christ, and thou shalt be saved'.*

"It was so real to me, that I found myself talking out loud to

Jesus: *'Lord, I am a great, a very great sinner';* and he replied, *'My grace is sufficient for thee'.*

"My doubts began to fight back. I replied, *'But, Lord, what is believing?'*

"And then I thought of John 6:35, and for the first time I realised that 'believing with my mind' was actually the same as 'coming to Jesus'. *He that came, that is, run out in his heart and affections after Salvation by Christ, he indeed believed in Christ.*

"I got a bit emotional and found myself saying: 'Can you really cope with someone as bad as me?' and he said to me the words of John 6:37: '**All that the Father giveth Me shall come to Me, and him that cometh to Me I will in no wise cast out**'.

"I remember it was late afternoon, and I could see some of the stallholders in the fair down below beginning to pack up.

I still had some problems, and I said: 'But Jesus, how must I think of you so that my faith in you is correct?' And he replied with a torrent of verses that came to my mind:

> **'Christ Jesus came into the world to save sinners'** (1 Timothy 1:15)
>
> **'For Christ is the end of the law for righteousness to everyone that believeth'** (Romans 10:4)
>
> **'(He) was delivered for our offenses, and was raised again for our justification'**(Romans 4:25)
>
> **'(He) loved us, and washed us from our sins in His own blood'** (Revelation 1:5)
>
> **'For there is one God and one mediator between God and men, the man Christ Jesus'** (1 Timothy 2:5)

**'Therefore He is able also to save to the uttermost those who come unto God by Him, seeing He ever liveth to make intercession for them'** (Hebrews 7:25).

"From all this I realised that *I must look for righteousness in his person, and for satisfaction for my sins by his blood*; everything that Jesus did in obedience to his Father was not for himself, but for anyone who will accept it *for his salvation, and be thankful.*

"I was overcome with a great sense of joy, my eyes filled with tears, and I actually felt a tremendous love for the *name, people, and ways of Jesus Christ."*

The Pilgrims sat in silence for a bit. Through the open door of the church they could hear a rather hesitant song thrush, and a sudden breeze brought in the smell of newly-mown grass.

CHRISTIAN looked at his friend. *"This was a revelation of Christ to your soul indeed; but tell me particularly what effect this had upon your spirit."*

HOPEFUL thought for a bit and then said: "I think it made me see the world, in spite of all the good things there are around, as being under the condemnation of God. But it also helped me see that although God is a God of Justice, he has a way to acquit the believing sinner.

"Understanding this made me really ashamed of the *vileness* of my former life, and I was overwhelmed by my sheer ignorance. Never before had I had thought of or sensed the *beauty of Jesus Christ.*

"It made me *love a holy life*. I longed to do something *for the honour and glory of the name of the Lord Jesus*. In fact, I thought that if I now *had a thousand gallons of blood in my body, I could spill it all for the sake of the Lord Jesus."*

# 36 IGNORANCE DISPLAYS HIS IGNORANCE

They walked out of the church, through the graveyard and back out on to the road.

*I saw, then, in my dream,* that HOPEFUL, turning round to follow the flight of a heron, spotted IGNORANCE coming over the brow of the hill behind them.

"Hey," he said, "young CitiBoy is way behind us and not eager to come closer."

CHRISTIAN stopped and looked back. "I don't think he likes us."

"We wouldn't have eaten him," said HOPEFUL.

"True," said CHRISTIAN, "though I expect he thinks we might."

"Probably, but let's wait for him to catch up," replied HOPEFUL.

Seeing a pub up ahead with a beer garden, they decided to wait for him there. In the corner of the bar was an out of tune piano, and an out of tune pianist was pounding out some golden oldies.

As IGNORANCE approached the pub, CHRISTIAN called over to him: "Come and have a drink with us; there is no need to walk alone."

IGNORANCE hesitated, but then went over to the table where

the Pilgrims were sitting. He put his copy of the FT on the floor and sat down.

"Take your jacket off," said Christian, "What can I get you?"

"A pint of Speckled Hen, please," he said. "Potatoes have jackets, gentlemen wear coats. Actually I prefer to walk alone, unless I like the people I'm with."

He took his coat off, revealing a pair of wide red braces. CHRISTIAN looked knowingly at HOPEFUL, but ignored the snub.

"Well, have a break and talk to us anyway for a bit. Work in the City, do you? Banker? Trader? Hedge Fund Manager? How does that affect your walk with God?"

"Research Analyst at Banque Inutile, actually," said IGNORANCE. "As far as God is concerned, I know he is always there helping me in my work."

"How can you be sure of that?" asked CHRISTIAN.

"Well, I think about God and heaven all the time."

"Really?" said CHRISTIAN, "but so do the *devils and damned souls*."

"Yes, I know that," said IGNORANCE lifting his pint. "Cheers. But I think of God and heaven constantly, and really want to know God more."

"So do many who are unlikely to get anywhere near heaven. Remember Proverbs 13:4: ***'The soul of the sluggard desireth, and hath nothing'***."

"Perhaps," said IGNORANCE, "but not only do I think constantly about God, I have left everything for the sake of heaven."

CHRISTIAN looked sceptically at the man's Paul Smith shirt, his Rolex and gold bracelet, and said: "You certainly seem to have brought quite a lot of it with you. Leaving everything is a tougher challenge than many realise. So why do you think you have left everything for God and heaven?"

IGNORANCE thought for a minute and put some Bombay Mix in his mouth.

"Well," he said, "it is because my heart tells me I have."

"Proverbs 28:26 says: **'Only fools would trust what they alone think'**," responded CHRISTIAN.

"But that is written about an evil heart," said IGNORANCE, "and *mine is a good one*."

"How can you prove that?" asked CHRISTIAN in surprise.

IGNORANCE replied confidently: "it *comforts me in the hopes of heaven*."

"But the heart is deceitful," said CHRISTIAN. "When you buy your lottery ticket, your heart tells you that this week you are definitely going to win, yet the statistics are all against you. And the statistics, of course, are right."

"But my feelings and my experience are at peace with each other, and therefore I believe my hope is well founded."

CHRISTIAN looked at him in amazement. "Who tells you your feelings and experience hang together?"

"Well, my heart does."

"Your heart does?" CHRISTIAN was staggered. "That's asking the jury to acquit the defendant on the basis of the defendant's evidence. Your heart tells you! I am afraid you need an independent witness, and in these matters it is only the evidence of the Word of God that counts."

"But a good heart has good thoughts, doesn't it? And surely a good life is one lived in obedience to God's commandments?"

"Agreed," said CHRISTIAN, "but it is one thing to have good thoughts and a good life, and another to think you have them."

"So what, in your opinion, are good thoughts, and what do you think constitutes a life lived in accordance with God's commandments?" asked IGNORANCE.

"Well, there are loads of good thoughts about God, Jesus and other things."

"Yes," persisted IGNORANCE, "but what are good thoughts about ourselves?"

"Thought that agrees with the Word of God, of course," replied CHRISTIAN.

"And when do our thoughts about ourselves agree with the Word of God?"

"When our assessment of ourselves is the same as the assessment of the Word of God," said CHRISTIAN. "Let me explain: the Word says that in our natural condition, nobody is righteous or does good, and our imaginations are continually evil. Look at Romans 3. So when we think of ourselves like that, then we have good thoughts."

IGNORANCE emptied his glass, and said: "I will never believe that my heart is bad like that."

"Let me get you another one," said CHRISTIAN.

"No, it's my round," said IGNORANCE. "I'll buy – same again?"

“Yes, please,” said CHRISTIAN, “and while you’re at it I’m going to write down the proper chords for ‘Strangers in the Night’ for the pianist, because I can’t stand it any longer. He may think he is doing a great job, but it’s not what the composer wrote.”

CHRISTIAN scribbled away on the back of a menu, and went over to talk to the pianist. IGNORANCE brought back the drinks.

# 37 DISCORD IN A MAJOR MISUNDERSTANDING

They carried on with the conversation.

“Well, I’m very sorry,” said CHRISTIAN, “but with respect I have to say to you that you have never had a good thought about yourself in your life.

“But let me go a step further. The Word passes judgment not only on our hearts but also on our lives. So when both are in accordance with the Word, then both are good.”

“What are you getting at?”

“Look,” said CHRISTIAN, “the Word of God says that *man’s ways are crooked ways; not good, but perverse.* Look at Psalm 125:5 and Proverbs 2:15 as well as Romans 3. It says that *they are naturally out of the good way, that they have not known it.*

“So when we think like that, humbly and sincerely, then we have good thoughts about our life because our thoughts agree with *the judgment of the word of God.*”

“And so what do you think are good thoughts about God?” asked IGNORANCE, beginning to look a bit irritated.

CHRISTIAN said calmly: “When our thoughts about God agree with what the Word says about him, then we know we have good thoughts about God. We must think of his being and attributes as the Word sets them out.

"There isn't really time to summarise what these are now, but we can say that we think of God rightly when we recognise that he knows us better than we know ourselves, and can see sin in us that we cannot see; when we think he knows our secret and hidden thoughts in the depths of our being; but also, when we think that all the good things in our hearts and lives are nothing to him but a bad smell, and that therefore we have no way of standing with confidence before him, however good our best actions may be."

"Do you really consider me stupid enough to think that God can see no further than I can, or that I would even contemplate standing before God on the basis of my good actions?" said IGNORANCE, angrily.

CHRISTIAN looked at him in surprise: "Well, what do you believe then?"

"To put it simply, *I think I must believe in Christ for Justification."*

"But how can you believe in him if you don't see that you need him?" countered CHRISTIAN, getting a bit worked up.

"If you cannot see any shortcomings in your life, so you cannot see any need for *Christ's personal righteousness* to justify you before God, on what basis do you say 'I believe in Christ'?"

"I have a real and worthwhile faith," protested IGNORANCE.

"And what is it?" asked CHRISTIAN, leaning forward with interest.

"*I believe that Christ died for sinners*," said IGNORANCE, "and that I shall be justified before God *from the curse, through his gracious acceptance of my obedience to his law*; in other words, Christ makes my good thoughts, good life and religious duties *acceptable to his Father by virtue of his merits, and so shall I be justified."*

“Wow,” said CHRISTIAN, sitting back in his seat, “Let me tell you what I think about that as a Gospel:

1. You won’t find that in the Bible

2. It’s rubbish because it relies on your righteousness for justification rather than Christ’s

3. It’s also rubbish because it makes Christ the justifier of your actions, not of your person, and indeed justifier of your person for the sake of your actions

4. In fact it’s complete rubbish, because it will not save you on the *day of God Almighty.* True saving faith accepts the righteousness of Christ. The soul that knows it is lost because of its failure to keep the law, flies to Christ for refuge in his righteousness.

“Think about it. This *righteousness of his is not an act of grace by which he makes for justification thy obedience accepted with God; but his personal obedience to the law in doing and suffering for us what that required at our hands*.

“It is this righteousness that true faith accepts; *under the skirt of which, the soul being shrouded*, is *presented as spotless before God, it is accepted, and acquitted from condemnation*.”

“Really? Is that what you think we should believe?” IGNORANCE sounded sceptical.

“You mean we should trust in what Christ did for us two thousand years ago when we were not even around? That’s a recipe for unbridled immorality: wine, women and song, why not? What does it matter how we behave if we can be accepted by God on the basis of *Christ’s personal righteousness* and all we have to do is believe this formula?”

"IGNORANCE by name, and ignorant by nature," said CHRISTIAN getting impatient. "Even your answer proves it. You have no idea what *justifying righteousness* is all about, and you haven't a clue about how to *secure thy soul, through the faith of it, from the heavy wrath of God.*

"You really have no idea at all about the *true effects of saving faith in this righteousness of Christ*: which is, *to bow and win over the heart to God in Christ, to love his name, his Word, ways, and people;* what a complete ignoramus you are!"

There was a chilly pause.

"This is about as interesting as an accountants' tea party," said Ignorance.

HOPEFUL asked IGNORANCE if Christ had been *revealed to him from heaven.*

IGNORANCE groaned and said: "I knew it, you're a revelations freak. People who talk like that have blancmange for brains. You're one stop past Dagenham, absolutely Barking."

# 38 RIGHT FEAR

"Don't be daft," said HOPEFUL. "You cannot see Christ with your physical eyes, so the only way you can have saving knowledge of Jesus is if God the Father reveals him to you."

"That may be your faith," said IGNORANCE, "but it is certainly not mine, and I think my faith is just as good as yours, but I don't have as many bonkers ideas in my head as you do."

"Let me say something," said CHRISTIAN. "This is serious stuff, and I completely agree with my friend that no one can know Jesus Christ except *by the revelation of the Father,* and the faith *by which the soul lays hold upon Christ* comes only through the *exceeding greatness of his mighty power*.

"And I see, my poor friend IGNORANCE, that your main ignorance is of the working of this faith. Wake up! Get a grip! Look at the true *wretchedness* of your human condition, and *fly to the Lord Jesus*; *and by his righteousness, which is the righteousness of God (for He himself is God), thou shalt be delivered from condemnation."*

The pianist had started on something that sounded like "Blame it on the Boogie" but his chord sequence in the chorus was driving CHRISTIAN to distraction.

"If he's playing in E Flat, it's not two lines of D Flat in the chorus, it's A Flat7/C Sharp and C SharpSuspended2," said CHRISTIAN. "We have to get out of here before I do something I regret."

IGNORANCE sat where he was, in something of a huff. "I've got a sore ankle. You walk so fast, I can't keep up," he complained. "You press on, but I want to rest for a bit."

CHRISTIAN and HOPEFUL set off down the road together. HOPEFUL started to sing 'Don't blame it on the sunshine…', but CHRISTIAN cut him off. "That brings back painful memories," he said, "let's do something else."

So they went down the road singing:

*"Well, IGNORANCE, Wilt thou yet foolish be,*
*To slight good counsel ten times given thee?*
*And if thou yet refuse it, thou shalt know*
*Ere long the evil of thy doing so.*
*Remember, man, in time; stoop, do no fear:*
*Good counsel taken well, saves; therefore hear*
*But if thou yet shalt slight it, thou wilt be*
*The loser, IGNORANCE, I'll warrant thee."*

"It looks like we're on our own again," said CHRISTIAN.

In my dream I saw the Pilgrims go striding off, and eventually IGNORANCE came out of the Pub and hobbled along at a distance.

"I feel a bit sorry for him," said CHRISTIAN. "*It will certainly go ill with him at last.*"

"Sadly, there are many in our town in the same situation – whole families, indeed whole streets, including pilgrims," said HOPEFUL. "And if that is true where we come from, what must it be like where he comes from?"

"Remember the Bible verses that talk about people being blinded in case they should see."

CHRISTIAN looked over his shoulder and walked closer to HOPEFUL. "But now we are on our own, what do you really think of people like this CitiBoy? Do you think they have never worried about their sins? Have they never been concerned that their moral failures might have some eternal consequence?"

"You're older than me: you can answer that question better than I can."

"Well," said CHRISTIAN, choosing his words carefully, "I think it is certainly possible. I think ignorance can prevent people from seeing that feelings of guilt are there for their benefit, so they desperately try to stifle them and continue to flatter themselves that their way is the right way."

"Actually, I agree with you," said HOPEFUL. "Fear can be an incentive to improve and put things right, and indeed can be a good thing, if it prompts people to start their pilgrimage."

"As my old granny often used to remind us: *'The fear of the Lord is the beginning of wisdom'.*" said CHRISTIAN.

"And how would your old granny describe a fear that is right and proper?" asked HOPEFUL.

"We were too afraid of her to ask her... but I think she would have said, coming from a good Brethren background, that true, or right, fear can be summarised by three points beginning with the letter 'R':

1. *By its **Rise**:* right and proper fear is caused *by saving convictions for sin.*

2. Right and proper fear ***dRives*** *the soul to lay fast hold of Christ for salvation.*

3. Right and proper fear gives birth in the soul to an ongoing **Reverence** *of God, His Word, and Ways;* it

keeps the soul sensitive and loyal, making it afraid to turn away to anything that may *dishonour God, break its peace, grieve the Spirit, or cause the enemy to speak reproachfully.*

"Good old granny: that seems pretty sound to me, but the second one does not begin with 'R'," HOPEFUL pointed out.

"Granny was a bit Rebellious, but she always pointed us to Christ the solid Rock."

"Hmm... Do you think we are past the Enchanted Ground yet?" asked HOPEFUL.

"Why? Are you bored with my conversation?"

"Not at all," protested his friend, "I just want to know where we are."

# 39 KEEPING YOUR EYE ON THE BALL

CHRISTIAN pulled out the map and studied it for a minute. "We have just under two miles to go," he said, putting it back in his pocket.

"But let's go back to the issue: ignorant people cannot see that fear is a positive. They do not see that feelings of guilt which lead to fear for the future are actually a great power for good, and so instead of responding to their feelings, they try to stifle them."

"How?" asked HOPEFUL.

"Four ways," said CHRISTIAN:

1. They assume that these feelings come from the devil (*though indeed they are wrought of God)*; and so they resist them as they see them as something destructive.

2. They think these fears will ruin their faith, when actually they do not have any faith to ruin; and so they suppress them.

3. They think that fear is for wimps, and so put on a pretence of confidence.

4. They see that these fears undermine their *pitiful old self holiness*; and so they resist them with all their might.

“That resonates with me,” said HOPEFUL, “*before I knew myself,* I was like that.”

“I think we should increase our distance from our neighbour IGNORANCE,” said CHRISTIAN, “so let’s jog the next bit.”

They took out their iPods, put on their headphones and set off running to music; HOPEFUL listening to Delirious and CHRISTIAN listening to Delius.

After a few miles CHRISTIAN slowed down as they as they approached a small village. They could see a cricket match in progress on the village green, and decided to stay and watch for a bit.

They bought a couple of Crabbies from a stall and sat down on the grass. The rather elderly bowler was taking his time, and the batsmen were both a bit timid, playing defensive shots.

“Let’s grapple with another Tough Question,” said CHRISTIAN pulling the top off the bottle with his teeth.

“Go for it,” said HOPEFUL, “but it’s still your choice.”

“OK, what about this one?” asked CHRISTIAN. “Do you recall a chap who lived in your part of the world, called TEMPORARY?”

HOPEFUL thought for a minute. “Yes, I remember him,” he said. “He had a flat in GRACELESS, a town about two miles from HONESTY, and he was in the same block as TURNBACK.”

“That’s the one,” said CHRISTIAN. “He came back from Soul Survivor hot as mustard, keen as cress. He seemed to have a real awareness of sin and its consequences.”

“Yes, I think he did,” said HOPEFUL. “I lived about three miles away, and he would often come round and pour his heart out. I was really sorry for him, and had hope for him; but as we know, *it is not everyone that cries, 'Lord, Lord!'*

"Well, one day he told me he wanted to go on a pilgrimage, just like us," said CHRISTIAN, "but then he struck up a friendship with SAVE-SELF, and after that I saw little of him."

"OK, I see," said HOPEFUL, "you want to talk about why some people suddenly lose their faith and enthusiasm and start back-sliding?"

CHRISTIAN smiled. "You've guessed it – I think it's really important, but you start."

"Alright," said HOPEFUL. "Why does it happen? Here are four possibilities:

1. **They have not thought it through:** their conscience may have been awakened, but their mind has not been convinced. So when the guilt begins to wear off, the thing that made them turn to religion is no longer there. So they go back to where they were, and the bit in 2 Peter 2:22 about dogs returning to their vomit springs to mind.

   When a dog is sick, it throws up not because it has thought about it (if a dog can think), but because it has gut rot and the stomach does what is natural. But once the gut rot is over, and the stomach returns to normal, *his desires being not at all alienate from his vomit, he turns him about and licks up all.*

   So, *being hot for heaven* simply because of fear of the torments of hell means that, as their sense and fear of *hell and damnation chills and cools*, so their enthusiasm for heaven and salvation cools also.

Once guilt and fear are gone, so does religious enthusiasm, and they are back to square one.

2. **They worry about what other people will think:** although they are *hot for heaven so long as the flames of hell are about their ears*, when that terror subsides, they have second thoughts.

They begin to think that it is better to be wise and not run the risk of losing everything, when they are not sure what they will gain.

Or they worry about bringing *unavoidable and unnecessary troubles* upon themselves, and so they gradually do what everybody else is doing.

3. **They think religion is rather degrading:** they actually think that religion is a crutch, or the opium of the less intelligent, and is *low and contemptible.* When they have lost their sense of *hell and the wrath to come*, their pride gets the better of them, and they go back to where they were.

4. **They actively suppress their feelings:** feelings of guilt and fear disgust them. While initially their guilt pointed them in the right direction, once they feel safe they become embarrassed.

Their embarrassment makes them suppress their feelings, and so they deliberately destroy the thing that has started them on their journey, and they go on to make choices that will further deaden their feelings.

"How does that sound to you?"

"That's a pretty good analysis," said CHRISTIAN, clapping as one of the batsmen was given out 'lbw'. A young girl, padded up, was walking confidently towards the crease.

"At root this is all about a change of both mind and will," he said. "It's a bit like a crooked accountant at the Old Bailey: in front of the judge and jury he is clearly afraid and penitent. But it is fear of a long time in clink, not remorse, that really drives his grovelling. Once free, he will most probably return to his old ways and continue to cook the books. Only if his mind has been changed will the outcome be different."

"OK, I have suggested the reasons for backsliding, the 'why' of a cooling of faith," said HOPEFUL, "so you explain the 'how', the way in which it happens."

"Right-ho," said CHRISTIAN, "it often goes like this:

1. They begin to stop thinking about God, death, and judgment to come.

2. Then they gradually ease off on the spiritual disciplines: private prayer, *curbing their lusts, watching, sorrow for sin, and the like*.

3. Then they stop meeting with *lively and warm Christians*."

The young girl was knocking the ball all over the field, and the villagers were almost getting excited.

"This is beginning to look lively and warm," said HOPEFUL, sitting up and watching the action.

CHRISTIAN ignored him, and went on:

"4. After that they *grow cold to public duty: as hearing, reading, godly conference, and the like.*

5. Then they begin to criticise mature Christians, and use their alleged short-comings as an excuse to dispense with religion.

6. Then they begin to keep company with *carnal, loose, and wanton men*.

7. Then they start gossiping and looking for evidence of hypocrisy in public figures and church leaders, and are glad when they find it and can use it as an excuse for their own lax behaviour.

8. After this they begin to *play with little sins openly*.

9. And so, having suppressed their feelings, they behave as they really are: and unless there is a *miracle of grace* to *prevent it,* they sink into a sea of misery and *everlastingly perish in their own deceivings."*

The young batswoman gave a swipe too far, and was out. There was a smothered groan from the spectators, but it was also time for tea, so the teams walked back towards the pavilion, and the Pilgrims got to their feet and set off down the road.

# 40 BEULAH LAND

*Now I saw in my dream* that the Pilgrims had at last left the Enchanted Ground, and were now entering the country of Beulah, where the air was sweet and pleasant.

Since the road led straight through this land, the Pilgrims spent time enjoying the surroundings. The bird life was incredible, the smell of the veldt invigorated them, new flowers appeared in the fynbos each day, and they heard the *voice of the Turtle in the Land*.

Beulah is a place where the sun shines, night and day. It is beyond the Valley of the Shadow of Death, and out of the reach of GIANT DESPAIR whose Doubting Castle could not even be seen. Here the Pilgrims were within sight of the City to which they were heading, and it was here that they met some of the inhabitants of Beulah, *Shining Ones* who regularly walked this country on the borders of heaven.

CHRISTIAN and HOPEFUL sat down on a grassy knoll beside a pond, and read together from Isaiah 62. Beulah is the land where God the Bridegroom renews the contract with his people, his Bride, and blesses them with his joy and happiness.

Here there is no shortage of *corn and wine*, and here the Pilgrims found in abundance all they had been looking for in their pilgrimage. When the wind was in the right direction they could hear voices coming from the City, quoting Isaiah, which was why the Pilgrims had stopped to look at this passage.

As they watched some weaver birds building a nest on a tree, the Pilgrims felt a greater sense of fulfilment and thanksgiving than they had ever experienced so far on their journey.

From their vantage point they had an excellent view of the City to which they were heading. The buildings and streets were of pure gold, and the walls and roofs were studded with pearls and gemstones, such that the reflection of sunlight and the *natural glory* of the City made CHRSTIAN feel ill *with desire*.

HOPEFUL, too, was struck with the same sickness, and the two of them lay in the grass crying out because of the pain of longing. HOPEFUL quoted from Song of Songs: *"If you see my Beloved, tell him that I am sick of love."*

"Not fed up with love, but ill with love," he pointed out.

After a while they felt able to get up and be on their way, and as they came closer to the City they walked through *orchards, vineyards and gardens*, whose gates opened onto the highway.

At the gate of one of the vineyards, a gardener was sitting eating his lunch. The Pilgrims asked him who owned the vineyards and gardens.

"They belong to the King," said the gardener through a mouthful of cheese and pickle, "and they are planted for his own enjoyment and for the sustenance of Pilgrims. When I've finished my sandwich I'll show you round and you can pick your own fruit."

The gardener showed them the *King's Walks*, and the *Arbours where he delighted to be*. The Pilgrims spent time walking around, and then slept soundly under the shade of the trees.

I noticed in my dream that they were talking in their sleep; they sometimes did this on the journey, but here they were doing it much more.

As I was wondering about this, the gardener looked straight at me and said, "What's the problem, dreamer? It's the grapes what does it – they cause the lips of the sleeping to speak."

When the Pilgrims woke up, they started to head towards their goal, but the sun reflected so brightly off the golden buildings that they couldn't look at the City without dark glasses. As they walked along the road with their shades on, they met *two men in raiment that shone like gold, also their faces shone as the light.*

These men asked the Pilgrims about their journey, the ups and the downs, and where they had stayed. "Well, you only have two more difficulties," they said, "and then you are in the City."

CHRISTIAN and HOPEFUL asked if the men would accompany them on the last stage. They said they would, but reminded the Pilgrims that each person's entrance to the City had to be obtained by his or her own faith. *So I saw in my dream that they went on together* until they came in sight of the gate.

Now I saw that between the Pilgrims and the gate was a very deep river, with no bridge. The Pilgrims were astonished, but the men told them they had to go <u>through</u> the river or they could not get to the gate.

"Is there no other way to the gate?" asked CHRISTIAN, who knew he was not a strong swimmer.

"Yes," said the men, "but since the beginning of the world only Enoch and Elijah have been allowed to go that way, and nobody else will be permitted until *the last trumpet shall sound.*"

The Pilgrims, and CHRISTIAN in particular, began to feel discouraged. They looked up and down the riverbank, but could find no ford across and no boat, lifebelt or buoyancy jacket to help them. HOPEFUL asked if the water was a uniform depth.

"No," said the men, "but we cannot be more specific. What we can tell you is that you will find it deeper or shallower in proportion to your belief in the King of the City."

Seeing that there was no alternative, the Pilgrims waded into the water. Straight away, CHRISTIAN began to sink. He shouted to his good friend, HOPEFUL, "I am sinking in deep water! I am being overwhelmed by *his* waves!"

"Hang in there!" HOPEFUL shouted back, "I can feel the bottom, and it is firm!"

CHRISTIAN cried out in agony, "My friend, my friend, the *sorrows of death* have me in their grip. I shall never see the land that *flows with milk and honey!"*

A great darkness and horror engulfed CHRISTIAN; he could not see anything in front of his face.

His mind began to give out, so that he could not remember or talk lucidly about the good things that had happened during his pilgrimage. All he could express was his terror that he would die in the river and his fear that he would never enter the gate.

It was clear to HOPEFUL and the onlookers that CHRISTIAN was agonising over the sins he had committed, both before and after he became a Pilgrim. He also seemed to be fighting off visions of *hobgoblins and evil spirits.*

Going to his aid, HOPEFUL had a hard time keeping his brother's head above water. He would vanish beneath the flow of the river, and re-emerge half drowned, while HOPEFUL was trying all the time to encourage him, shouting: *"Brother, I see the gate, and men standing by it to receive us!"*

But CHRISTIAN answered: “No, it’s you they are waiting for, not me: you are the one who has been hopeful ever since I knew you!”

“*And so have you!”* yelled HOPEFUL at CHRISTIAN, pulling him up again by his jacket.

“No, no, my brother,” CHRISTIAN cried out, “if I was worthy, those on the other side would come and rescue me; but my sins have brought me into this trap and there is no hope for me.”

And he tried to sink down beneath the water to drown himself.

## TIME FOR A COFFEE BREAK

Do you think of old age as being on the borders of heaven?

How do you feel about your inevitable death?

How has CHRISTIAN changed during his pilgrimage? How have you changed through your pilgrimage so far? What further changes do you hope for?

What expectations should we have of older people in the church? Does godly wisdom always come with increasing years?

Does it matter if a person comes to faith through fear of death and hell? Is fear a more effective motivator than love? If so, should this affect the way the church presents the Gospel?

Why has the Church lost its missionary zeal? Do we perhaps think that ignorance may be better at Judgment Day than having heard the Gospel and rejected it?

Given the limited resources we have, which is our priority: helping the maximum number of people to faith in Jesus, or growing fewer but more effective disciples?

What sort of spiritual care should the Church offer to those whose minds no longer function?

As bodily appetites decrease with age, old people have less incentive to commit traditional sins. What are the sins of old age?

How will you maintain hope when your body has pretty much given up?

What will stay with you from your reading of Pilgrim's Progress?

# 41 CROSSING THE RIVER

"Pull yourself together," said HOPEFUL yanking him back up again.

"Come on, my brother, you have quite forgotten what Psalm 73 says of the wicked: **'For there are no bands in their death, but their strength is firm. They are not in trouble as other men; neither are they plagued like other men.'**

"Your agonies in these waters are not a sign that God has abandoned you, but are sent to test whether or not you will count your past blessings and trust God in your struggles and difficulties."

*Then I saw in my dream* that CHRISTIAN stopped struggling, and seemed lost in thought.

HOPEFUL said to him, *"Be of good cheer, Jesus Christ maketh thee whole."*

And with that CHRISTIAN suddenly shouted out, "Oh yes! I see him again! And he tells me, *'When thou passest through the waters, I will be with thee; and through the rivers, they shall not overflow thee'."*

*Then they both took courage, and the enemy was after that as still as a stone, until they were gone over.*

CHRISTIAN found a firm foothold on the riverbed, and after that they found the rest of the water was shallow.

*Thus they got over.*

As they climbed on to the riverbank on the other side, they were greeted by the two shining men who had been waiting for them.

“We are *ministering spirits*,” they said to the Pilgrims, “sent to help and support those who will be *heirs of salvation*."

Together they walked up the hill towards the gate.

The City stands upon a steep hill, but the Pilgrims climbed up easily, because they had the *two men to lead them up by the arms*, and also because they were stark naked with no clothing to restrict them.

They had left their *mortal* clothing behind them in the river, and so they sped up the hill like Greek athletes, even though the foundation upon which the City was built was *higher than the clouds*. Up they went, *through the Region of the Air*, talking as they went, relieved that they had come safely through the river and had such *glorious companions to attend them.*

The Pilgrims asked the Shining Ones about the *glory of the place* on the other side of the gate, and were told that the *beauty and glory of it was inexpressible*. It is the *Mount Zion, the heavenly Jerusalem; the innumerable company of angels; and the spirits of just men made perfect.*

“You are going now,” their companions said, “to the *Paradise of God*, and you will see the tree of life, and eat of its never fading fruits. You will be given white robes and you will walk and talk with the King every day of eternity. Never again will you see the sorrow, sickness, affliction and death that you saw in *the lower region upon the earth*: those former things are passed away.

“You are going now to Abraham, to Isaac, and Jacob, and to the prophets; men that God took away from *the evil to come, and that are now resting upon their beds, each one walking in his righteousness."*

They could see the gate clearly now ahead of them. The Pilgrims asked, "What are we supposed to do there in that holy place?"

The Shining Ones answered: "You will receive the *comfort of all your toil, and have joy for all your sorrow; you must reap what you have sown, even the fruit of all your prayers, and tears, and sufferings for the King by the way.* There you *must wear crowns of gold*, and enjoy the *perpetual sight and visions of the Holy One*; for there you will see him as he is.

"It is one continuous worship there, praising the one you wanted to serve in the world, but without the limitations of the flesh.

"Your eyes and ears will be delighted with the sight and sound of the *Mighty One*. There you shall enjoy meeting your friends again, those who have come here before you, and you will joyfully receive all those who follow after. You will be kitted out with *glory and majesty*, and given riding gear so you will be fit to *ride out with the King of Glory*.

"When he comes with trumpets in the clouds, on the wings of the wind, you will come with him! And when he sits on the Throne of Judgment, you will sit beside him! And when he passes sentence upon all the *workers of iniquity,* whether *angels or men,* you also will have a voice in that Judgment, because they were enemies of both of you. And finally, when he returns to the City, you will go too, with the sound of the trumpet, and be with him forever."

As they approached the gate, a great crowd of the *heavenly host* streamed out to meet them. The Shining Ones held up the arms of the Pilgrims and proclaimed to the crowd, "*These are the men that have loved our Lord when they were in the world, and that have left all for his Holy Name; and he hath sent us to fetch them, and we have brought them thus far on their desired journey, that they may go in and look their Redeemer in the face with joy.*"

The crowd cheered and whistled and clapped and someone near the front started a song that was picked up and passed back: "*Blessed are they that are called to the marriage supper of the Lamb*".

Some of the King's trumpeters, in shining white uniforms, came out through the gate to join the singing crowd moving towards the city, and together they made the sky ring with melody and sound.

The trumpeters sounded a ten thousand welcome salute, heralding the arrival of CHRISTIAN and HOPEFUL from the world: and the crowd clapped and cheered even more, surrounding the Pilgrims with love and care and song as they guided them towards the gate. It looked as if heaven itself had come down to meet them!

They continued up the hill as the singers and musicians, mixing anthems and instrumentals with hugs and laughter, showed how much they welcomed CHRISTIAN and his brother Pilgrim into their fellowship, and how much joy this celebration was giving them.

For the two men, it was like being in heaven before they had actually arrived there, and they were overwhelmed by the sight of the angels and their beautiful harmonies.

# 42 THROUGH GATES OF SPLENDOUR

At last the City was before them, and they thought they could hear every bell ringing to welcome them, but what encouraged them most was the thought that they would be living with these loving and happy people for ever and ever. *Oh, by what tongue or pen can their glorious joy be expressed! And thus they came up to the Gate.*

Looking up at the Gate, the Pilgrims saw written over the archway in letters of gold some words from the Book of Revelation: *'Blessed are they that do his commandments, that they may have right to the tree of life and may enter in through the gates into the City.'*

In my dream, I saw the shining men telling them to knock at the Gate, and when they did, Enoch, Moses, and Elijah and others looked over the doors and asked who they were. The Shining Ones shouted up: *"These pilgrims are come from the city of Destruction, for the love that they bear to the King of this place."*

Each Pilgrim handed over his Roll, which they had received *in the beginning;* these were taken to the King, who, when he had read them, asked, "Where are these men?"

He was told they were standing outside the gate.

The King then commanded that the gate be opened, quoting Isaiah, so *"that the righteous nation that keeps truth, may enter in".*

Still in my dream, I saw the two men enter through the gate, and as they stepped over the threshold, they were *transfigured*; they found themselves with new clothes that shone like gold. Another crowd arrived to meet them, carrying a gift of harps and crowns which they gave to the Pilgrims: a harp to use in praise, and a crown as a sign of honour.

*Then I heard in my dream* that all the bells in the City rang again for joy, and the crowd shouted: *"Enter ye into the joy of your Lord!"*

I even heard CHRISTIAN and HOPEFUL singing loudly: "*Blessing, honour, glory, and power, be to him that sitteth upon the throne, and to the Lamb for ever and ever".*

When the gates opened to let the men in, I caught a glimpse inside myself, and I could see that the City shone like the sun: the streets were indeed paved with gold; and in them walked *many men, with crowns on their heads, palms in their hands, and golden harps to sing praises withal.*

Some of the men had wings, and were continually saying to each other: *"Holy, holy, holy, is the Lord!"* And then the Gates were slowly shut behind the Pilgrims, and I was left wishing that I could be there inside with them.

While I was reflecting on all of this, I looked around and saw IGNORANCE arriving at the riverbank. He had no problem in getting across, because he had spotted a ferry down river. VAIN-HOPE, the ferryman, rowed him across, and he walked on his own up the hill to the gate.

Nobody came to greet him.

When he reached the gate, he looked at the inscription, and knocked, expecting the doors to be opened immediately.

Some men appeared on top of the gatehouse and looked down at him.

"Where have you come from?" they asked. "And what do you want?"

IGNORANCE replied: "I have wined and dined in the presence of the King, and he has *taught in our streets*."

They asked him for his Roll, his certificate, to show to the King. He fumbled around in his coat pockets, but could not find anything.

The men on the gate asked: "Haven't you got one, then?" IGNORANCE stood still and said nothing.

So they told the King. The King would not come down to see IGNORANCE, and ordered the two Shining Ones who had escorted CHRISTIAN and HOPEFUL to the City, to go out, and seize IGNORANCE, bind him hand and foot, and get rid of him.

They lifted him under the armpits and carried him through the air to the door that I saw in the side of the hill, and threw him in there. *Then I saw that there was a way to hell, even from the gates of heaven, as well as from the city of Destruction.*

So I awoke, and behold it was a dream!

## THE CONCLUSION

***Now, reader,*** *I have told my dream to thee;*
*See if thou canst interpret it to me,*
*Or to thyself, or neighbour: but take heed*
*Of misinterpreting; for that, instead*
*Of doing good, will but thyself abuse:*
*By misinterpreting evil ensues.*

*Take heed also that thou be not extreme*
*In playing with the outside of my dream;*
*Nor let my figure, or similitude,*
*Put thee into a laughter or a feud.*
*Leave this for boys and fools; but as for thee,*
*Do thou the substance of my matter see.*

*Put by the curtains, look within my veil*
*Turn up my metaphors, and do not fail*
*There, if thou seekest them, such things to find*
*As will be helpful to an honest mind.*

*What of my dross thou findest there, be bold*
*To throw away; but yet preserve the gold.*
*What if my gold be wrapped up in ore?*
*None throws away the apple for the core.*
*But if thou shalt cast all away as vain*
*I know not but 'twill make me dream again.*

***End of Part One***

Yes, patient Reader, I am afraid that was only Part One. In Part Two you meet Mr Great-Heart, Mr Standfast, and Mr Valliant-for-Truth. You also meet the women.

I sometimes joke that when John Bunyan got back from prison with his manuscript, Mrs Bunyan sent him off with a flea in his ear and told him that his story was far too sexist, and he must write a sequel that rebalanced the gender levels.

Part One of Pilgrim's Progress was published in 1678, and Part Two at the end of 1684. John was in prison for twelve years from 1660-72 and again from December 1676 to June 1677. John died in 1688, Elizabeth, his second wife, died in about 1691, and there is plenty about John on the internet.

John had been warned that there was a warrant out for his arrest, and he could have avoided capture. He chose to suffer imprisonment, believing that this was what God wanted him to do. In *Grace Abounding* he writes about the distress this caused him: *"The parting with my Wife and poor Children hath oft been to me in this place, as the pulling the flesh from my bones… O I saw in this condition I was as a man who was pulling down his house upon the head of his Wife and Children; yet thought I, I must do it, I must do it."*

Part One has much about the (male) individual's journey, while Part Two is not just about the female journey, but about the journey of the group, the church.

Before I start doing a similar job on Part Two, it would be very helpful to know if you found Part One helpful. What worked for you? What did not work? Did it help you on your journey in any way? Do you think it would help any of your friends, and is it a helpful resource for a home group discussion?

Please let us know on **info@CHGRL.org**, and we will put up the comments on the CHGR website **www.CHGRL.org**. Christians can be pretty hurtful while proclaiming that they are speaking the truth in love, so when you email some criticism, please make sure you run it past Jesus first.

# BIBLE REFERENCES

1. **A Man in a Mess:** Isaiah 64:6, Luke 14:33, Psalm 38:4, Habakkuk 2:2, Acts 16:30-31, Hebrews 9:27, Job 16:21-22, Ezekiel 22:14, Isaiah 30:33, Matthew 3:7 and 7:13-14, Psalm 119:105, 2 Peter 1:19, Luke 14:26, Genesis 19:17, Jeremiah 20:10, 2 Corinthians 4:18, Luke 15:17, 1 Peter 1:4, Hebrews 11:16, Luke 9:62, Hebrews 9:16-22, Hebrews 13:20-21

2. **Everybody Needs Good Neighbours:** Titus 1:2, Isaiah 45:17, John 10:27-29, 2 Timothy 4:8, Revelation 3:4, Matthew 13:43, Isaiah 25:8, Revelation 7:16-17, and 21:4, Isaiah 6:2, 1 Thessalonians 4:16-17, Revelation 5:11, 4:4, and 14:1-5, John 12:25, 2 Corinthians 5:2-5, Isaiah 55:12, John 7:37 and 6:37, Revelation 21:6 and 22:17

3. **Bogged Down:** Psalm 40:2, Isaiah 35:3-4, 1 Samuel 12:23(?)

4. **Advice from an Estate Agent:** 1 Corinthians 7:29

5. **The Hazardous Hill:** Exodus 19:18, Exodus 19:16, Hebrews 12:21, Hebrews 12:25, Hebrews 10:38, Matthew 12:31, Mark 3:28, 1 John 4:5, Galatians 6:12, Luke 13:24, Matthew 7:13-14, Hebrews 11:25-26, Mark 8:34-35, John 12:25, Matthew 10:39, Luke 14:26, Galatians 4:21-27 and 3:10, Psalm 2:12, Matthew 7:8

6. **The Keeper of the Wicket Gate:** John 6:37, Matthew 7:14

7. **The Interpreter:** Across 17th Century Europe 'Emblems' (pictures with verses or Tableaux) were very popular. Bunyan's 1688 Emblem book was called 'A Book for Boys & Girls'
   **The Art Gallery:** 1 Corinthians 4:15, Galatians 4:19, 1 Thessalonians 2:7
   **True Dirt:** Romans 7:9, 1 Corinthians 15:56, Romans 5:20, John 15:3, Ephesians 5:26, Acts 15:9
   **The Tryptych:** Romans 16:25-26, John 15:13, Luke 16:19-31, 2 Corinthians 4:18
   **An Interactive Display:** 2 Corinthians 12:9
   **The Courtyard Tableau:** Acts 14:22
   **The Prisoner:** Luke 8:13, Hebrews 6:6, Luke 19:14, Hebrews 10:28-29
   **The Film Clip:** 1 Corinthians 15:51-52, 1 Thessalonians 4:16-17, Jude 15, 2 Thessalonians 1:8, John 5:28, Revelation 20:11-14,

Isaiah 26:21, Micah 7:16-17, Psalm 5:1-3, Daniel 7:10, Malachi 3:2-3, Daniel 7:9-10, Matthew 3:2 and 13:30, Malachi 4:1, Luke 3:17, 1 Thessalonians 4:16-17, Romans 2:14-15
**So What Did You Make of That?**

8. **The Cross:** Isaiah 26:1, Zechariah 12:10, Mark 2:5, Zechariah 3:4, Ephesians 1:13

9. **Approaching Difficulty Hill:** Proverbs 23:34, 1 Peter 5:8, John 10:1, Galatians 2:16, Isaiah 49:10, Proverbs 6:6

10. **The Palace Beautiful:** Revelation 3:2, 1 Thessalonians 5:7-8, Mark 13:34, Genesis 9:27

11. **Piety, Prudence & Charity:** Hebrews 11:15-16, Romans 7:14-24, Isaiah 25:8, Revelation 21:4, Genesis 19:14, 1 John 3:12, Ezekiel 3:19

12. **About the Lord of the Hill:** Hebrews 2:14-15, 1 Samuel 2:8, Psalm 113:7, Hebrews 11:33-34, Isaiah 33:16-17

13. **Apollyon:** Romans 6:23, Micah 7:8, Romans 8:37, James 4:7

14. **The Valley of the Shadow of Death:** Jeremiah 2:6, Numbers 13, Psalm 44:19, Psalm 107:14, Job 3:5 and 10:22, Jeremiah 2:6, Psalm 69:14, Ephesians 6:18, Psalm 116:4, Psalm 23:4, Job 9:11, Amos 5:8, Job 12:22 and 29:3

15. **Faithful's Story:** Proverbs 15:10, 2 Peter 2:22, Genesis 39:11-13, Proverbs 22:14, Proverbs 5:5, Job 31:1, Ephesians 4:22, 1 John 2:16, Romans 7:24

16. **Moses the Merciless:**

17. **Shameless:** 1 Corinthians 1:26 and 3:18, Philippians 3:7-9, John 7:48, Luke 16:15, Mark 8:38, Proverbs 3:35. The Royal Society had been recently founded in 1662.

18. **Talkative:** Matthew 23:1-3ff, 1 Corinthians 4:20, Romans 2:24-25, James 1:22-27, Matthew 13:1-50 and 25:1-46, Leviticus 11:1-8, Deuteronomy 14:3-8, 1 Corinthians 13:1-3 and 14:7

19. **What's so Obvious about Grace?:** Genesis 39:15, 1 Corinthians 13, John 16:8, Romans 7:24, John 16:9, Mark 16:16, Psalm 38:18, Jeremiah 31:19, Galatians 2:16, Acts 4:12, Matthew 5:6,

Revelation 21:6, Romans 10:10, Philippians 1:27, Matthew 5:9, John 14:15, Psalm 50:20, Job 42:5-6, Ezekiel 29:43(?)

20. **One of You is Going to Die:** John 4:36, Galatians 6:9, I Corinthians 9:24-27, Revelation 3:11. "We shall this day light such a candle by God's grace in England, as I trust shall never be put out." 1555, quoted in Foxe's *Book of Martyrs.*

21. **Vanity Fair:** Isaiah 40:17, Ecclesiastes 1:2-15 and 2:11,17, 1 Corinthians 5:10, Matthew 4:8, Luke 4:5-7, 1 Corinthians 2:7-8, Psalm 119:37, Philippians 3:19-20, Proverbs 23:23, Hebrews 11:13-16. Ben Jonson's comedy Bartholomew Fair (1614) included a Jacobean Puritan, Mr Zeal-of-the-Land Busy.

22. **The Trial:** Exodus 1, Daniel 3, Daniel 6. A 'pick-thank' is someone who flatters or curries favour.

23. **Hopeful Joins the Team:** Proverbs 26:25. A 'by-end' is a secondary consideration; 'prating' is chattering, empty talk.

24. **Gossip with a Columnist:** a 'gripe' was a miser or usurer; think Scrooge.

25. **The Bishop and the Actress:** a 'stalking horse' is one that you hide behind when hunting.

26. **Get Rich Quick:** Hosea 4:18(?), 2 Timothy 4:10, 2 Kings 5:20, Matthew 26:14-15 and 27:1-6, Genesis 19:26, Numbers 26:9-10, Genesis 13:13, 10

27. **By-Path Meadow:** Psalm 65:9, Revelation 22:1-2, Ezekiel 47:1-12, Psalm 23:2, Isaiah 14:30, Numbers 21:4, Isaiah 9:16, Jeremiah 31:21

28. **Doubting Castle:** Psalm 88:18, Job 7:15. 'Diffidence' is not reticence, but want of faith or confidence, mistrust.

29. **With One Bound they were Free:**

30. **The Delectable Mountains:** John 10:11, Hosea 14:9, Hebrews 13:1-2, 2 Timothy 2:17-18, Proverbs 21:16

31. **The Mugging of Little-Faith:** Proverbs 26:12, Ecclesiastes 10:3, Matthew 12:45, Proverbs 5:22, 1 Peter 4:18, 2 Timothy 1:14, 2 Peter 1:9, Hebrews 12:16, Genesis 25:32, Jeremiah 2:24

32. **Be Prepared:** 1 Peter 5:8, Job 41:26, Job 39:19-25, Ephesians 6:16, Exodus 33:15, Psalm 3:5-8, Psalm 27:1-3, Isaiah 10:4. Psalm 88 is ascribed to Heman.

33. **Some Tough Discipline:** Proverbs 29:5, Psalm 17:4, Proverbs 29:6, Daniel 11:32, 2 Corinthians 11:13-14, Romans 16:18, Deuteronomy 25:2, 2 Chronicles 6:26-27, Revelation 3:19, Jeremiah 22:13(?), Ecclesiastes 10:15, 2 Corinthians 5:7, Proverbs 19:27, Hebrews 10:39, 1 John 2:21, 1 Thessalonians 5:6

34. **The Enchanted Ground:** Ecclesiastes 4:9, Romans 6:21-23, Ephesians 5:6, Isaiah 64:6, Galatians 2:16, Luke 17:10

35. **Faithful Explains the Good News:** Hebrews 10:12-14, Romans 4:22-25, Colossians 1:15-20, 1 Peter 1:3-9,21, Matthew 11:28, Matthew 24:35, Psalm 95:6, Daniel 6:10, Jeremiah 29:12-13, Exodus 25:22, Leviticus 16:9, Numbers 7:89, Hebrews 4:16, Habbakuk 2:3, Ephesians 1:18-19, Acts 16:30-31, 2 Corinthians 12:9, John 6:35, 37, 1 Timothy 1:15, Romans 10:4, Romans 4:25, Hebrews 7:24-25

36. **Ignorance Displays his Ignorance:** Proverbs 28:26, Romans 3:9-20, Genesis 6:5

37. **Discord in A Major Misunderstanding:** Psalm 125:5, Proverbs 2:15, Romans 3:23

38. **Right Fear:** Matthew 11:27, 1 Corinthians 12:3, Ephesians 1:18-19, Job 28:28, Psalm 111:10, Proverbs 1:7, 9:10

39. **Keeping Your Eye on the Ball:** 2 Peter 2:22, Proverbs 29:25

40. **Beulah Land:** Isaiah 62:4, Song of Songs 2:10-12, Isaiah 62:5, 8 and 11-12, Deuteronomy 23:24, Revelation 21:18, 2 Corinthians 3:18, 1 Corinthians 15:51-52,

41. **Crossing the River:** Psalm 73:4-5, Isaiah 43:2, Hebrews 12:22-24, Revelation 2:7, 3:4 and 21:1, Isaiah 57:1-2 and 65:14, Galatians 6:7, 1 John 3:2, 1 Thessalonians 4:13-16, Jude 14, Daniel 7:9-10, 1 Corinthians 6:2-3, Revelation 19:1-10

42. **Through Gates of Splendour:** Revelation 22:14, Isaiah 26:2, Revelation 5:13-14

# OTHER UPDATED VERSIONS

**E. W. Walters (1938):** Sub-titled 'Arranged for the Modern Reader'. Some 'Thees' and 'Thous' but sticks very closely to the text. It does away with the Play format of some of the dialogue in the original. No illustrations. (Duckworth)

**James H. Thomas (1964):** 'In Today's English', but maintains the dialogue format of the original. By-Ends becomes 'Crafty', Giant Despair becomes 'Gloom'. The songs/poems are omitted, and there are a few sort of period drawings. (Moody Press) (Also Kingsway 1994 with colour illustrations)

**Geoffrey T. Bull (1969):** "As I staggered on through the grey death of the post-Hiroshima era .." and he amplifies the text considerably, but it does make it much more readable. If you think I have overdone the embellishment, try this one. Vanity fair is now called Sexpo. (Hodder & Stoughton)

**Jean Watson (1978):** For Family Reading, all the heavy dialogue omitted, and Puritan style drawings on every page. (Scripture Union/Galley Press)

**Hal M. Helms (1982):** Readable, but a bit stilted in parts so not entirely 'modernized' as it says on the label. Mid-19th Century wood engravings of Puritans, and Notes and References at the end of each chapter. (Paraclete Press)

**Warren Wiersbe (1989):** "The New Pilgrim's Progress" but the format is much like the original, although the language is updated. This version is heavily annotated, not just with references but also with commentary on the theology. (Discovery House/Moody Bible Institute)

**Dan Larsen (1989):** Billed as a re-telling, but actually a fairly good précis. Interesting treatment of the Flatterer, which is a good test of any modern version. Plenty of drawings, but Puritan-style characters. (Barbour Publishing)

**Lynne Howles (1993):** *'The King's Highway',* a Play for children in nine Scenes. Starting in the Village of Doldrums, Christian, his sister Faith, and their friend Fairweather set off to the Great City. (Morley's Print & Publishing)

**Dick Worth (1994):** Cuts down some of the dialogue, and retains the Play format in parts. More an abbreviated than a modernized version, and has a few Puritan-style line drawings. (Pilot Books)

**Gary D. Schmidt (1994):** A précis, omitting Talkative and Ignorance, as well as Hopeful's testimony. Illustrations are a mixture of periods, and the author admits some of the thoughts and reactions are his own. (William B. Eerdmans)

**L. Edward Hazelbaker (1998):** The English generally reads well, and the Play format is abandoned. Some phrases of Bunyan remain and seem a bit incongruous, for example: "Then tears stood in my eyes. ..' is not what we would normally say in Modern English. (Bridge-Logos)

**James Pappas Jnr (1999):** 'The New Amplified' version, and this is certainly obvious at the foot of the cross where the conversation with the three Shining Ones goes well beyond Bunyan; not sure about the branding iron. Occasional Puritan illustrations. (Destiny Image)

**Geraldine McCaughrean (1999):** A heavily abridged version, but one of the few with some humour in it. You meet Pluto Crat and Miss Stake, but the Key to get out of Doubting Castle is not called Promise so something important is lost. The drawings are different from the usual. (Hodder Children's Books)

**Sovereign Grace (2000):** No named adaptor, 'Pilgrim's Progress in Modern English', but only up to a point, Lord Copper. No divisions into chapters, no illustrations, Play format retained. (Sovereign Grace Publishers)

**Lael Arrington (2002):** Generally follows Bunyan's story, but admits it is a re-creation rather than a re-telling. American Chris becomes Christian at the Cross, and this is a very 21st Century background. (NavPress)

**Tim Dowley (2004):** Amazed to find my old University mate was working the same seam. A re-telling for children, with good modern illustrations. It is a précis of all the important events, but obviously omits the theological dialogues. (Lion/Candle Books)

**EasyRead Edition (2006):** No named adaptor, but this is essentially the original in modernish English, Play format, but large typeface. (Objective Systems PTY)

**Helen L. Taylor (2006):** Little Pilgrim's Progress, originally a serial in a children's magazine, set in a children's world and follows the original faithfully. Apollyon becomes Self, and the illustrations are Puritan. (Moody Publishers)

**Tim Dowley & Steve Smallman (2008):** A Board Game for 2-6 players, the aim is to be first through the gate into the Celestial City. It comes complete with Despair and Progress Cards, and the Atheist Despair Card sends you back to the beginning. (Lion/Candle Books)

**C. J. Lovick (2009):** Commended by Jim Packer and Tim Dowley, Puritan-style illustrations, sticks to the text but is as readable as you can make it without trying to add un-Puritan colour or interest. (Crossway)

**Peter and Anne Woodcock (2009):** A CD with a ninety-minute recording telling the story in seven sessions, comes complete with an Activity Book for children. (DayOne Publications)

**Dreamstairway (2010):** No named editor, but halfway between the original and modernish English. Puritan illustrations, some 'thees' and 'thous'. (Dreamstairways Classic Tales Series)

**Lee Tung and Johnny Wong (2011?):** Comic Strip version, but only goes as far as the end of the valley, Pope and Pagan being the last page. Loved it, but then I'm only an Engineer. (Kingstone Comics)

# ACKNOWLEDGMENTS

If you want to read the original, the Penguin Classics version is probably the best. This reflects the scholarship of Rogers Sharrock and Pooley, and there are some useful Notes and some suggestions for further reading. However, I found two bits of dialogue and a line of a poem missing, and the references do not seem to have been checked. So I also used the Oxford World's Classics version edited by W. R. Owens as a double check. Even there the references were not quite right, and I have listed three with question marks that I have not been able to work out.

Thanks to the Chaplins for letting me lie on their lounge floor during a St Andrews Quiet Day and re-discover Pilgrim's Progress from Jane's father's library. Special thanks to Kate Miller for improving my writing style, making it less office memo and more readable. Also thanks to those who have read the drafts: Jorj Kowszun, Hannah Kowszun, Heather Lane, Mark Overton, Philippa Probert, Sue Mulligan, Rebecca Willis, Corinne Aldis, Nick Thornton, Alice Instone-Brewer, Jane Chaplin, and Matthew Penson. And very special thanks to Viv for letting me ruin many holidays by banging away on the laptop when we should have been out walking.